Under Her Spell

Eliza Daly

To Christine,
I hope you enjoy Monica and Reed's story!
Happy reading!
Eliza Daly

CRIMSON ROMANCE
Avon, Massachusetts

This edition published by
Crimson Romance
an imprint of F+W Media, Inc.
10151 Carver Road, Suite 200
Blue Ash, Ohio 45242

www.crimsonromance.com

ISBN 10: 1-4405-5733-0
ISBN 13: 978-1-4405-5733-0
eISBN 10: 1-4405-5734-9
eISBN 13: 978-1-4405-5734-7

Dedication

FOR MY HUSBAND MARK, FOR BELIEVING IN ME WHEN I SOMETIMES DIDN'T BELIEVE IN MYSELF. WITHOUT YOUR UNWAVERING SUPPORT, MY DREAMS MAY NEVER HAVE COME TRUE. LOVE YOU.

Acknowledgments

Thank you to my husband, family, and friends, for believing in me and helping me maintain my sanity on this roller coaster ride to publication. To my mom, Judy Watson, for reading all my books—often numerous times—and being a grammar guru. Jill Wood Lawrence, critique partner extraordinaire, and one of my biggest cheerleaders. Kate Bowman, for being a first reader and having faith in this story. Laura Iding, for all the brainstorming sessions over a few glasses of wine. Fellow Crimson author Elle J Rossi, for recommending I submit my book to Crimson Romance. And thank you to everyone at Crimson Romance, especially Jennifer Lawler, for believing in this book and making the process so easy.

Prologue

Monica Jackson was raising a bowl of sea salt, preparing to cast a spell circle on her bedroom floor when the door flew open. She nearly dropped the bowl as her cousin Hope stormed in, covered with flour and cake batter—the Unhappy Homemaker from Hell.

"No way is he getting the BMW," Hope said, shaking a wooden spoon in her hand and sending batter flying across the room.

The night before, Hope had caught her scumbag husband Kyle in bed with another woman. Not wanting to impose on her happily married friends, she'd showed up at Monica's door, even though they weren't exactly close. Hope made a Stepford Wife look like a total slacker, and the only thing she and Monica had in common were their Italian features: dark hair and brown eyes. A wedding cake decorator, Hope was coping with Kyle's infidelity by baking like a mad woman. Forget the cake. Monica would shove *Kyle* in the oven and roast him on high.

"What are you doing?" Hope's gaze narrowed on the small wooden table in front of Monica, where the ingredients for her soul mate spell sat on top of a red tablecloth: a red candle, lavender incense, jasmine oil, cinnamon, and a love letter to her as yet unidentified true love.

"Casting a spell to help find my soul mate."

"A spell? Does that really work?"

"Hopefully."

Monica's psychic friend Jordan had convinced her that spell casting was a viable alternative to Milwaukeemates.com and speed dating in general. Neither of which Monica had time for, since establishing her new business was top priority. Her company, Enhance Your Romance, planned unique romantic events and was sure to succeed, unlike her other dozen failed business plans. Society was obsessed with being in love.

"A spell . . . " Hope mused, then her face lit up. "If there's a spell to attract a man to a woman, there must be one to repel women from a man. Right?"

"Spells shouldn't involve negative energy. Sending out negative energy can cause it to return threefold. They aren't intended to harm someone or make them do something against their will." Jordan had drilled this into her head.

"I wouldn't be making Kyle do anything against his will. I'd be warning *women* to stay away from *him*."

Sounded borderline.

"Please," Hope whined, picking a clump of batter from her long, wavy hair.

Monica let out a defeated groan. "All right." Hope would never actually cast the spell anyway. When they were young, Hope refused to wear a Casper costume for Halloween because she didn't believe in ghosts. She was closed-minded when it came to paranormal or New Age beliefs. And you had to truly believe in a spell for it to work.

Monica set down the bowl of salt and grabbed a pencil and pad of paper off her desk and handed them to Hope. "Write this down. It's called," she tapped a hot pink nail against her lip, "the dirtbag spell."

"Like it already." Hope jotted down the title as she perched on the edge of the bed's purple floral comforter.

"Take one of Kyle's socks, fill it with dirt, and add a photo of him. It's critical you aren't in the photo." Monica paced, tightening the sash on her lavender silk robe. "Include something of his like . . . "

"His new Rolex?"

Personally, Monica would list the watch on eBay and pray for a bidding war. But Hope, no matter how ticked off, was too timid to sell Kyle's precious watch, and too frugal to risk damaging it by mixing it with dirt.

“That’s fine. Sew up the sock and bury it in your front yard. It’ll warn all women he’s a dirtbag.”

Hope poised the pencil against her lower lip, reviewing the spell. “Don’t I have to say something when I bury it, like a chant?”

What happened to being spell ignorant?

“Bury it in the moonlight while saying . . . ” Monica scrambled for a few rhyming lines, “moonlight, glowing bright, warn all women in your sight, the man who lives in this house, is a dirtbag and a total louse.”

“Perfect.” Hope sprang from the bed, looking inspired. “Kyle’s at work. I’m going over to the house right now to bury that sock.” She turned and marched out, a woman on a mission.

Monica nibbled nervously on her fingernail. Hope wouldn’t seriously go through with casting the spell, would she? A big part of spell casting was psychological, focusing all your energy on making something happen. Monica had never seen Hope look so determined, or vindictive. Hopefully, if she did cast the spell, the negative energy didn’t return threefold.

What was the worst that could happen?

Chapter One

One Week Later

It was after eight a.m., and Monica was definitely running late. She grabbed a white cotton blouse from her closet and dug a pair of pink capris out of the hamper. She hung the clothes on the back of the bathroom door and when she'd finished showering, the wrinkles had virtually disappeared. At least the capris didn't look like they'd been rolled in a ball ten minutes earlier. Concealer did little to hide the dark circles under her eyes, so she gobbed on mascara to distract from them.

Once again, Hope had kept her up until the wee hours of the morning, eating chocolate, lemon, carrot, and a few unknown kinds of cake and plotting ways to destroy Kyle's life. Monica should have been brainstorming engagement proposal ideas for a client rather than adding five pounds to her butt.

Monica zipped downstairs and into the kitchen to grab a Frappuccino.

Hope stood over the stove, looking perky in her yellow floral sundress—only her bloodshot eyes betrayed the two-hour crying jag she'd had before going to bed. Her emotions were all over the place. "I'm making eggs Benedict."

Mmm . . . The aroma of melted butter and hollandaise sauce made Monica's stomach growl. She was already late, so another fifteen minutes was no big deal. She glanced down at the button threatening to pop on her capris. She'd skip lunch.

Hopefully, their living situation was temporary. Besides needing to rid her home of Hope's cooking and negative energy, Monica wanted rid of her cousin's cows grazing all over the kitchen. From the cow magnets on the fridge, to the cookie jar that mooed when you opened it, the entire kitchen was done in country crafty crap and blue and white gingham.

Yet, she could hardly kick Hope out when the townhouse belonged to their grandparents. Last month, when the couple retired to Florida, Monica had moved into their groovy retro pad. The kitchen, done in yellow and orange, opened up into the dining room, painted a bright red. Her grandma had left psychedelic patterned drapes on the patio doors, along with the appliances and an electric blue sofa with lime green daisies. Not having the funds to decorate, Monica had only contributed a small TV, a computer, and her bedroom set, allowing plenty of room for Hope's stuff.

The phone rang on a pedestal table in the dining room and Monica grabbed the receiver.

"Monica, ya bitch!" the man on the other end roared.

"Ah, Kyle?" She should have looked at the caller ID.

"You're not getting away with this."

"Wanna clarify that?"

"You know damn well what I'm talking about. My cell phone's dead and I just got home to find a half dozen messages on my machine checking to see if I'm alive. My mom about had a heart attack when she read my obit in the paper."

Eight in the morning and he was just getting home? What a slime. Wait a sec, she hadn't sent Kyle's obit to the newspaper. She glanced over at Hope fidgeting with a metal spatula and nibbling at her lower lip. Whoa. Quite assertive for Hope. No wonder Kyle assumed Monica had done it.

"Yeah, well too bad it didn't give *you* a heart attack." Monica slammed down the receiver and looked at Hope. "I can't believe you put Kyle's obit in the paper."

"I know, it was immature. I did it in the heat of the moment. But better than running him over six times with my car, crushing every bone in his pathetic body, so he's in excruciating pain and a body cast for years." A flicker of doubt shone in Hope's eyes and

Monica made a mental note to hide the woman's car keys. Better that Hope lived with her than in the state pen.

"I'm not saying it was the *wrong* thing to do. I just can't believe you did it. So what did he die of?"

"Necrotizing fasciitis."

"What's that?"

"A flesh-eating disease."

Monica grimaced. "Sounds perfect."

*

It was almost nine when Monica pulled her powder blue scooter up in front of her office, located in an old brick building on Milwaukee's trendy Eastside. Jordan's friend, a corporate real estate agent, had rented her the space for a steal when the previous tenant vacated overnight, leaving behind a mess and no forwarding address. Monica agreed to clean up the office and take over the lease through the end of the year. If she hadn't landed such a great deal, she would have been working out of her home. Right now, Hope would be sewing a blue gingham cushion for Monica's desk chair and advising her clients on the negative consequences of romance and marriage.

Monica lifted the seat on her scooter. She removed her purse and purple briefcase then stuck her helmet in. As she walked toward her office, she foofed her shoulder length hair and read the specials board in the window of Chico's Mexican restaurant, reminding herself that she was skipping lunch. An early dinner was always a possibility.

The song "As Time Goes By" sang out above the door as she walked into her business. Monica thought it more welcoming than a jingling bell, and it tied in with the vintage *Casablanca, Gone with the Wind* and *Sabrina* movie posters on the wall. Comfy red upholstered chairs invited clients to sit down and relax while waiting.

Now, she just needed people to sit in them.

Her friend slash assistant, Jordan, sat at her desk, tarot cards laid out in front of her.

"Looks like business is booming," Monica said.

Gaze narrowing, Jordan slid a pair of lime green glasses on top of her head, sweeping back the sides of her short bob—a light brown with streaks of pink. "You look like hell."

"Thanks. Good to know I look as bad as I feel. I was up all night again with Hope."

"If anyone is keeping you up all night, it should be some hot guy, not your cousin. And yes, business *is* booming." Jordan smiled wide, snatching a pink note off her desk and handing it to Monica. "You spoke to some guy last week at the Brewers game about getting engaged at a Packers game. He's stopping by around ten. Didn't get his name. His girlfriend must have come into the room since he hung up on me."

That would make only two bites from the engagement proposal Monica had conducted at the Brewers game. The sold-out stadium held over forty thousand people. Where were all her new clients? She'd done just six events in two months, but after that baseball game, she'd been certain her company was about to take off.

"I don't think that career spell is working," Monica said.

"Oh ye of little faith." Jordan tapped a gold nail against a tarot card on her desk. "The Ace of Pentacles means financial reward is on the way." She flipped the card around so it was right side up.

"Why'd you turn that around?" Monica had had enough readings to know there was a different meaning if the card was upright or reversed. "Upside down means I'm financially screwed, doesn't it?"

Jordan let out a defeated sigh, looking busted. "You are not financially screwed. I'll lend you more money if you need it. No big deal."

Jordan ran a lucrative psychic business and worked part-time helping Monica get her business up and running. Since graduating from college seven years ago, many of her friends had achieved successful careers and had joined Jordan in investing in Monica's business. One day they would see a hefty return on their money. Her friends had faith in her, and for that, she was forever indebted.

"That's okay, I have money," Monica assured her.

If her credit cards weren't all maxed out.

Jordan grabbed her purse. "I'm making a latte run. You want one?"

"Whatever has the most caffeine in it."

Jordan breezed out the front door.

Monica walked into her office. She booted her computer, scanning the slew of pink sticky notes lining the perimeter of the monitor. One reminded her to buy more sticky notes, several others had ideas for future events, and one noted an appointment that afternoon with a girl from the Brewers game, who wanted to propose to her boyfriend at the upcoming French festival.

Monica snatched up the smiley face foam ball on her desk and tossed it between her hands, brainstorming ideas. The girl could perform in the can-can dance and then at the end lift her skirt and have *Will you marry me, Tom?* written across her frilly undies. Very sexy, and unexpected, but was it romantic enough?

Fifteen minutes later, Jordan returned and Monica decided to run out and buy a French music CD for inspiration. Sitting on her scooter, she turned the key and pressed the ignition button. Rather than humming to life, it sputtered, then died. Great. She'd just bought it three months ago from a college kid, who now owned a brand new reliable Mustang. She couldn't afford any major repairs. No way was she going back to borrowing her dad's pickup truck with a yellow hard hat on top that read *Jackson Construction.* Talk about bad for a girl's self-esteem.

"Come on," she pleaded, rubbing a loving hand over the handlebars. "Don't do this to me, Frankie." She'd named the scooter after old blue eyes himself, Frank Sinatra, since the blue scooter had a retro look, and she was obsessed with swanky fifties lounge music. "Come on baby, please start." She tried starting it again, but nothing.

Her fingers tightened around the handle bars then relaxed as she started softly singing "The Way You Look Tonight," one of her favorite Sinatra tunes. "Yes, you're lovely . . . and your cheeks so soft . . . but to love you . . . " She swept her fingertips lightly down the shaft of the bike and back up. " . . . your tenderness grows . . . and that laugh . . . "

Noticing someone watching her out of the corner of her eye, she straightened, glancing over at a tall, dark-haired guy. He had on a boring black designer suit, but with a lavender-striped oxford and coordinating tie. Her favorite color. An amused smile curled the corners of his mouth. A dimple creased his cheek and lines crinkled around his blue eyes.

How long had he been standing there watching her serenade her scooter and practically feeling it up?

"Do you work here?" He gestured toward her office.

She nodded, sliding off the scooter and stepping onto the sidewalk next to him. "I'm Monica Jackson." She removed her large white sunglasses and slipped a bow down the front of her shirt. His gaze remained glued on her sunglasses. She glanced down at the glasses weighing down her shirt's neckline, exposing the tops of her breasts.

His gaze darted up and met hers. Busted. Yet, he didn't look the least bit embarrassed or apologetic. "Reed Walker. I was just coming to see you."

Oh, the Packers fan, a half hour early. A client. Figured. Gorgeous, sexy, a stylish dresser . . . too good to be single. Every guy who walked through her office door was either married or looking to get married and already had the prospective bride in mind. This definitely wasn't a job for finding a husband.

"Problems with your scooter?" he asked.

She glanced over at it. "I have no clue what's wrong. Drove it to work a half hour ago and now it won't start."

Thoughts of her dad's pickup truck caused her entire body

to tense. She took a calming breath, inhaling the scent of Reed's cologne, the essence of jasmine and something exotic. Had to be *Eternity*. Mmm . . . Her body slowly relaxed. She stopped just shy of inhaling another deep breath. Get a grip. The guy was a client. And he really wasn't her type. He was too perfect with his crisply ironed oxford and pressed suit. A total control freak no doubt. She couldn't picture him at a Packers game downing beer, dressed head-to-toe in green and gold, cheering the team to victory.

"I had a scooter like this in college," he said. "Not baby blue, or I'd have gotten my ass kicked on a daily basis. It was black." He stared reminiscently at the bike, sweeping a strong hand across the seat. "Sold it after I graduated. Sort of miss it."

"I'd let you take it for a ride, if it were running."

"Probably just a bad plug and now it's flooded. I'll take a look at it."

She studied his pressed suit jacket, unable to find a speck of lint or the slightest wrinkle. "I don't want you to get all dirty." She certainly didn't want him upset over ruining a designer suit and taking his business elsewhere. Although, there wasn't another romantic event planning company in the city.

So why didn't she have more business?

Reed smiled, slipping off his jacket. "I won't. If you could just hold this."

He held out his jacket and Monica took it, wanting desperately to slip it on and cover herself in the scent of jasmine. Jasmine was the best. She used it in all her spells.

Wait a sec, besides jasmine, lavender was also a key ingredient in her soul mate spell and this guy was wearing the color lavender. Were these signs? He couldn't be her man if he was already involved with someone else. Was this the universe's idea of a cruel joke, or merely a coincidence?

Monica carefully draped the jacket over her forearm, massaging the material—a silk blend—between her fingertips. Faint wrinkles appeared on the jacket and she quickly smoothed a hand over them. Reed rolled up his sleeves and she gawked at his muscular forearms. If he could stare at her breasts, she could admire his arms. He lifted the scooter seat and removed a small plastic tool bag attached to the underside. She'd forgotten that was even there. He took out a socket wrench.

"So, did you go to college around here?" she asked.

"Marquette."

He obviously had some dough, or major student loans.

He popped the side panel off the scooter and set it carefully on the street next to him.

"Wow, I didn't know that came off."

Rather than looking at her like she was a total ditz, he kindly gave her an overview of the engine and how to check the oil. She nodded with interest, hoping he couldn't tell her eyes were glazing over.

"I went to UW-Milwaukee," she said.

For a year, before she'd dropped out to pursue her business idea for *Singles Day*. A day to celebrate singledom. To gather with friends at fancy restaurants and exchange gifts or cards—a line of which she'd designed. Unfortunately, every major, and obscure, greeting card company had rejected her idea. Rather than going back to college, she'd worked a slew of temp jobs and started planning her next business venture.

"Used to work at Marco's by UWM." With each crank of the wrench, his arm muscles flexed then relaxed, and Monica inhaled an appreciative breath. "You ever go there?"

"Oh, yeah, Marco's." Marco's was a hole-in-the-wall true Italian restaurant and bar. By eight o'clock at night, the regulars were plowed on Sambuca and singing along to Tony Bennett and Dean Martin on the jukebox. "He makes the best Capellini Toscana. Reminds me of my grandma's. She makes her pasta from scratch."

Monica rarely even made pasta out of the box. She had every delivery restaurant on the Eastside on speed dial. According to her grandma, that was why Monica hadn't yet landed a man. Her grandma claimed her cooking, filled with love and a fair amount of Chianti, was partially responsible for fifty-two years of marriage. However, Monica's mom could barely make a frozen pizza and had just celebrated her thirtieth wedding anniversary. So she figured long marriages ran in the family DNA, even if good cooking skills didn't.

"You must be Italian. My grandmother made her pasta from scratch also."

"You're Italian?" She studied his bright blue eyes and fair skin, which barely showed a hint of a tan.

He nodded. "My grandmother was born in Tuscany."

Be still her heart. Her mom would buy her a new scooter if she brought home an Italian guy. For years her mom had been unsuccessfully fixing her up with the sons of her bocce ball partners at the Italian Center. Monica's last blind date showed up in a satin disco-era shirt and a red Trans-am with flames painted down the side. Not only had that been her last blind date, but her last date period, six months ago.

Quite depressing.

But this guy . . . was a client! Talk about bad for business if she started breaking up their relationships. She couldn't afford to lose a client. They were even more difficult to find than boyfriends.

Reed removed the spark plug from the engine. He stood, bringing the plug to his mouth, blowing on it several times. When he lowered it, a blotch of grease remained below his bottom lip. Monica stepped toward him and brushed a finger gently over the spot. Their gazes locked, her finger still below his lip. She continued brushing it back and forth as if she couldn't get rid of the stubborn spot. She wanted to let her finger trace over his lips then along his strong jaw line, and the tiny scar that was likely this guy's only flaw. The corners of his mouth curled into a smile, and she smiled in response.

"A spot of grease." She lowered her hand. "It's gone."

"Thanks." He glanced down at her hands. "Nice nails. Do you have a file? I need it to clean out the plug."

She grabbed her purse from inside the scooter's seat, rummaged through it, and finally produced a file.

Using the file, he meticulously scraped the gunk out of the plug. Before putting the plug back in the engine, he pressed the ignition button. "Need to clean the gas out of the cylinder." He put the plug back in, then once again attempted to start the scooter. It hummed to life.

Monica practically did a tap dance. "Thank you so much. This is wonderful. Don't know what I'd have done if you hadn't come along."

"You'll still need to replace the plug. There's an auto supply store up the street. If you want to pick one up, I can replace it for you."

"That'd be great. I at least have to buy you lunch for doing all this." She eyed the grease on his hands. "Sorry about that. I'll go get a cloth."

"No big deal. I'll get one from my office." He gestured toward the building behind them, next to hers.

Monica turned and her gaze landed on a sign in the window.

Marriage isn't a word, it's a sentence. I'll set you free.

She glanced up at the sign over the door. *Reed Walker: Family Law.*

Focusing on Chico's lunch specials when she'd driven up, she'd failed to notice the new signs. "A divorce lawyer?" she muttered in disbelief. Her gaze darted over to the guy. "You're a *divorce* lawyer? I thought you were a client." Being attracted to a divorce lawyer was much worse than a client. Suddenly his eyes didn't seem as blue and his arms looked wimpy. No way was he Italian. Or her soul mate. And what kind of straight guy wore lavender!

"A client?" He laughed as if that was the most ridiculous thing he'd ever heard. "Ah no, I just started moving in and stopped by to introduce myself."

"You have to take down that sign." Monica pointed at his window.

"It's my company motto. Helps attract business."

"Maybe for you."

He arched an amused brow. "That's the idea."

"You can't promote divorce." She clutched his suit jacket, crumpling it in her hand.

"I'm not promoting it. It's a fact of life. I don't have any control over the average marriage lasting seven years, or that one in every two ends in divorce."

Monica's gaze skittered around frantically as she searched for a response that didn't involve whipping the socket wrench through his window and mauling the sign to shreds. She spied a black Mercedes parked up the street. The license plate read *No Mer-ce.*

"Is that your car?" she demanded, pointing at the Mercedes.

He nodded, wearing a cocky grin. "Would you like to take it for a spin?"

She glared at Reed's car then over at him, hand on hip. "You obviously have a relationship phobia, afraid of marriage."

The smile vanished from his face and his look turned serious. "I'm not afraid of marriage. I'm all for it. If people didn't get married, I wouldn't have a job."

She put a death grip on his jacket, scrunching the material up in her hand. "You're such a . . . lawyer." A gazillion nasty lawyer nicknames and she couldn't think of *one* she was so flippin' mad. Eying his jacket crumpled in her hand, he looked slightly peeved. "Can I have that?"

She thrust the jacket at him.

He took the jacket and shook it out. "What are you so worried about? Doesn't bother me being next door to a business that promotes romance and marriage." He slipped on the jacket, then swept a hand firmly down a sleeve, attempting to smooth out the wrinkles.

"If somebody wants to get divorced, seeing my company isn't going to change their mind. But if my clients see *your* sign and have any doubts about getting married, which most guys do, they might back out on an engagement proposal."

"If they're that easily swayed, they shouldn't be getting married in the first place. They'd just be coming to see me in another year or so."

He was right, which ticked her off even more. "Not if you aren't here!" She spun around and stormed toward her office.

"I'm guessing lunch is off," he called after her.

Smug bastard. Heart racing, hands balled into fists at her side, she marched inside. She bolted past Jordan on the phone and into her office. She scooped up the smiley face foam ball on her desk and whipped it against the wall. She began pacing back and forth in front of the desk.

His sign was huge. It might as well be done in pink neon lights. You could see it all the way down the block. And think of the clientele he would bring in. Scorned, negative, down-on-love people like Hope. She'd probably be able to hear them bitching about their spouses through the walls.

She threw open her top desk drawer and spied a yellow folder containing a business plan for her next prospective venture, should this one not succeed. She worked on it in her spare time. Jordan had scolded her last week when she'd discovered it in the drawer, claiming Monica was attracting negative energy.

Maybe she was right.

She snagged the folder and stuck it in the bottom drawer, then slammed the drawer shut. Instead, she snatched up the small charm bag Jordan had made off her desk top and squeezed the life out of the gold silk bag, which contained the herb hawthorn to ensure success, a jade stone for prosperity, cinnamon, and her business card, sprinkled with a few drops of jasmine—what *used* to be her favorite essential oil.

Although Tinker Bell had sprinkled Wendy with pixie dust, if Wendy hadn't believed she could fly, she would have leapt out the window and plunged to the ground. Pixie dust was a spell tool, same as herbs and oils, to keep one focused on achieving a goal. But *belief* was the core ingredient. If Monica believed she could soar, she would.

She would succeed. She would succeed . . .

Yet, picking herself up and brushing herself off each time she confidently *leapt* out that "window of opportunity" into a new business venture, only to have it never materialize or immediately fail, was becoming more and more difficult. This business *had* to succeed.

She shoved the bag in her front pants pocket.

What had she done to deserve a divorce lawyer next door to her? She was a good person. She worked hard to bring love and happiness into people's lives. She never hurt anybody . . .

The dirtbag spell.

Had she sent negative energy into the universe and now it was returning threefold? Was that really possible? Would Reed Walker put her out of business? Would her soul mate die in some horrific accident before she had the chance to meet him? Leaving Hope and her to grow old together, roomies forever?

A sharp pain pierced her chest and she sucked in some serious air, clutching her chest as Jordan walked in.

Jordan rushed over to her. "What's wrong?"

"Can't . . . breathe," Monica sputtered.

Jordan ran out to her desk and returned with a McDonald's bag. She sat Monica down in a chair and held the bag over her mouth. "Take a deep breath and let it out slowly."

Monica's breathing was coming in rapid, shallow gasps. She inhaled a deep breath, along with the lingering aroma of an egg and cheese biscuit. After several deep breaths, her breathing was almost back to normal. She lowered the bag from her mouth. "What was that about?"

"A panic attack," Jordan said, matter-of-factly.

Monica shook her head. "No way. I've never had a panic attack in my life. I'm so not the type to have panic attacks."

"Was it a sharp stabbing pain that felt like a heart attack?"

Monica nodded reluctantly. *Omigod.* "It's that spell. I have to undo that spell." She quickly explained the dirtbag spell she'd cast on Kyle and about the divorce lawyer next door.

Jordan shook her head vigorously, looking totally freaked out, sliding her glasses on top of her head. "Did I teach you nothing? You can't undo a negative spell. The backlash can be even greater. Some people might disagree, but I would never cast a banishing spell."

"The spell on Kyle wasn't intended to outright harm him and is keeping him from hurting other women, so the good outweighs the bad. Doesn't it?"

Jordan slipped her glasses back down on her nose. "Even spells for the greater good can have negative consequences. You cast the spell without Kyle's permission. You shouldn't tamper with the free will of another person."

"I didn't even cast it, Hope did," Monica wailed.

Jordan slid the glasses back on top of her head, her forehead scrunched up in contemplation. The constant repositioning of her glasses was a sure sign she was stressing. "But *you* created it. I don't know." She twirled a clump of hair around her finger. "Well . . . I guess the spell doesn't have to be negative. It can simply be to protect you from evil and negative energy."

"Whatever it takes to get rid of Reed Walker."

"Reed Walker is the divorce lawyer next door?" Jordan's green eyes darted anxiously to the front window, as if hoping to catch a glimpse of the man.

"You know him?"

"I wish." Jordan hiked up the straps of her bra, exposing her large breasts along the scooped neckline of her lime green top. "*Milwaukee Beat* voted him one of the city's most eligible bachelors like six months ago. Some chick at a charity benefit paid five grand to have dinner, and who knows what else, with him." Jordan looked all gaga over this guy. "He's totally hot. He's—"

"Way bad for business." Monica batted Jordan's hand away from her breasts as she adjusted them in her bra. "What about Alan?"

"What about him? Two years and I don't see no diamond," she said, fluttering her ring-less finger. Her shoulders slumped and she let out a frustrated groan. "But you're right. We're meant to be together. It's in the stars. I just have to get that *into* Alan's thick head."

"Reed Walker won't be around much longer anyway."

"I don't see him going anywhere. He's a kick-ass divorce lawyer. Has a reputation as a real pit bull."

Generally, Monica admired anyone who had enough drive and dedication to establish such a successful business. But not in Reed's case. She wanted him out of business. Or at least *out* of the building next door.

Chapter Two

Early that afternoon, Monica sat in her office typing up a proposal for the Packer client, who'd finally showed up around noon. His tardiness was forgiven since he'd hired her.

Jordan flew into her office. "Vincent Bartolli just pulled up in a Jaguar and went into Reed Walker's office. He must be getting divorced."

Vincent Bartolli, owner of Bartolli Construction, was a ruthless bastard, rumored to have ties to the mob, which Milwaukee had worked hard for decades to run out of town. Thanks to this guy, Monica's dad's construction company had lost a city contract that almost put him out of business. The man had local officials in his pocket so he landed every city job.

Monica stalked out into the lobby and Jordan followed. They glared out the window at the black Jag. A few minutes later, Vincent Bartolli strode out of Reed's office, dressed in a designer suit, looking like an arrogant prick and royally pissed off. Unlike her dad's rough, sun-damaged skin—from years of outdoor work—this guy had smooth, fair skin. He undoubtedly left the manual labor to his employees. He got in his car and sped off.

"I cannot believe he's representing that jerk," Monica fumed.

She bolted out the door and flew over to Reed's office, nearly taking his front door off the hinges. She marched past the empty receptionist desk and into the office where Reed sat behind a large mahogany desk filled with orderly stacks of files and papers. A wooden penholder held a dozen identical gold pens. No scattered sticky notes, stray paper clips, or anything to give it the slightest hint of disorganization.

He glanced over at her, looking as ticked off as Vincent Bartolli had. He pushed his chair back from the desk and stood. "Can I help you?"

She marched over, stopping mere inches in front of him,

inhaling his jasmine scented cologne. She took a step back, yet stood her ground, squaring her shoulders, preparing for battle. "You have no morals representing a man like Vincent Bartolli. It makes you no better than him. Just because a high profile case like this can keep you in Armani suits until you retire is no reason to take it. I can't believe—"

"I'm not representing him," he said firmly. His top lip curled back in a sneer and contempt filled his eyes, which suddenly looked even bluer than before.

Her gaze narrowed. "Then what was he doing here?"

"Asking me *not* to represent his wife."

Her shoulders relaxed slightly. "You're representing his wife? But he's a very powerful man."

"So am I." His confident tone said *Bring it on Vincent Bartolli,* as did the muscles tensing his angular jaw.

"He could make your life a living hell." What was with her sudden concern over Reed Walker's welfare?

"I plan to make *his* life one. It's what I do best."

No doubt. The confidence this guy exuded was even sexier than his piercing blue eyes or the incredible body undoubtedly hidden under that pressed suit. She would kill for an ounce of it. He wasn't worried that this mob guy could probably pull strings and put Reed out of business or send him floating in the Milwaukee River. Reed planned to stand up for Vincent Bartolli's wife when a lot of other divorce lawyers wouldn't dare go up against him. Most importantly, if Vincent Bartolli lost his fortune and were put out of business, Monica's dad wouldn't be.

Consumed with gratitude and spontaneous by nature, she impulsively sprung up on her tiptoes and leaned forward, preparing to kiss his cheek to say *thank you.* She stopped just shy of following through with the kiss, mere inches from his face, close enough to count the eyelashes framing his gorgeous blue eyes and the ultra-fine lines on his lips. Omigod, she couldn't kiss this guy. Yet, she remained poised on her tiptoes, gaze glued to his lips. They looked soft and so freakin' kissable. She forced her gaze up, meeting his.

He lowered his head, bringing his lips to hers. His lips were soft and warm, the kiss gentle. He slipped his tongue in her mouth and she instinctively responded, sweeping her tongue across his, deepening the kiss. The taste of spearmint filled her mouth.

He placed his hands on the sides of her waist and she lowered her heels back to the floor as her body melted against his. Oh man, he felt good. She slipped her hands beneath his suit jacket, splaying them across his chest. It was rock solid, strong, stoic . . . incredible.

Backing up against the desk, she knocked over a stack of files. The phone shrilled out, vibrating next to her butt, and she jumped. Reed drew back slightly, staring into her eyes, their breathing labored. Their gazes exchanged a slew of nonverbal questions: *Should he pick it up? What if he didn't? How far would this go?*

The phone stopped ringing.

Their gazes still locked, her questions started taking another path. What was she doing kissing a guy who was against love, commitment, and everything she valued and her business stood for? He apparently saw the panic in her eyes and took a step back. She removed her hands from his chest, slipping out from between him and the desk, stepping away.

"This, ah, doesn't change how I feel about you." She brushed a finger over her lips, warm and swollen from the kiss.

His gaze traveled from her mouth, down over her breasts to the sliver of stomach showing where her shirt had slid up. "I thought you *felt* great."

This guy was a divorce lawyer. A divorce lawyer . . .

She tugged down the bottom of her shirt, covering her stomach. "You shouldn't have kissed me."

"Thought it was rather mutual."

"Well, it wasn't. And I still want you out of here."

She still wanted him on top of his desk with his clothes off. She had some serious issues here. She blamed her temporary insanity on a fleeting sense of gratitude, combined with the scent of jasmine fogging her brain's ability to think clearly and those damn blue eyes blinding her good judgment.

It wouldn't happen again.

*

Reed debated telling Monica he was only there temporarily while his new office in a high-rise downtown was being finished, but he liked seeing her fired up. The way her cheeks flushed and her brown eyes lit up when she was making her case, she'd have made a helluva trial lawyer. Or rather a lobbyist, fighting to save committed relationships on the verge of extinction. Totally delusional, but passionate about her cause.

And rather than smelling of some expensive perfume like most women he dated, she smelled like cinnamon, and tasted more refreshing than a double martini after scoring a huge client settlement. Which wasn't nearly as huge of a turn on as the fact that she wanted to get rid of him. Now *that* was damn sexy. Usually women tried to get him to stick around, at least until the sun came up. Especially since he'd been named one of Milwaukee's most eligible bachelors. What a joke.

He was far from eligible.

"So why'd you take his wife's side?" she asked.

He eyed the prominent dip above her upper lip, fighting the urge to run the tip of his tongue over it. She had a killer mouth. "That's client confidentiality."

"You must really hate Vincent Bartolli to go up against him."

Understatement of the year.

"Maybe I just like a challenge."

She tilted her head to the side, studying him, as if she could read him. He shifted his stance, uncomfortable with the thought that she could.

"I doubt you took her on out of the goodness of your heart."

Her comment stung. Which was insane. He wanted people to think he was a heartless SOB who only cared about the kill and money. It was good for business. But more so than money, he cared about justice. Especially in Natalie Bartolli's case.

"I took her on for the money. Same reason you take on your clients. We're not non-profit organizations."

"But my job brings people closer together, not further apart. It makes people happier."

"I guarantee you when Natalie Bartolli ends up with a settlement over fifty million, she'll be happy as hell."

"Money can't buy happiness."

"Money can buy anything."

"It can't buy me."

He arched a skeptical brow. "You sure about that?"

She gave him a disgusted look. "Yes, I'm sure." But the doubt in her eyes begged to differ.

"You're telling me you'd be just as happy if your business went bankrupt than if it became the city's premier romance broker?"

"That's not the same. Everyone needs money to survive. I'm just saying I don't need expensive cars and suits to be happy." She shot his Armani a disapproving glance then her expression softened. "Yet, I doubt you're really happy." She turned and walked out. Her tone, laced with pity rather than sympathy, bugged the hell out of him. He didn't want either from her.

So what exactly *did* he want from Monica Jackson?

Chapter Three

An hour later, Monica sat at her desk, typing furiously on her computer, still fuming about Reed's comment. She could not be bought, no matter how much she needed money. She was nothing like that man.

Brushing a finger across her lips, her mind flashed back to their kiss. Her stomach fluttered and she slapped a hand over it. She shoved the thoughts aside for the dozenth time.

"As Time Goes By" sang out in the outer office. Jordan was off buying sticky notes and other office supplies, so Monica walked out to greet Albert, an older gentleman who was surprising his wife with a balloon ride for their fortieth anniversary.

"Was in the neighborhood and thought I'd drop off a check," Albert said.

A loud crash sounded outside. Monica and Albert rushed out the front door. A blond woman in her forties, wearing a floral sundress and wielding a golf club, had just taken out the windshield of a red Corvette parked at the curb. She was preparing to demolish the driver's side window when Reed and a middle-aged man in a business suit bolted out of Reed's office.

"What the hell are you doing, Marjorie?" the man roared.

"You always wanted me to take up golf, Stan. I'm taking up golf."

Monica shot Reed a desperate glance. *Do something!*

He looked at her like she was nuts and no way was this woman using him to practice her drive.

Monica glared at him, then took a step toward the woman. "Please put that down," she said calmly.

Marjorie smiled sweetly. "Gladly." She put the club down, right through the driver's side window. Stan stormed toward her, but backed off when she raised the club. "Fifteen years of tolerating your snooty country club friends and listening to you bitch about your job and what do I get? Divorce papers."

"Along with our twenty-four-year-old gardener and—"

The shattering of glass drowned out Stan's protest as Marjorie sent the golf club through the rear window. She wound up to take another swing and the club slipped from her hands and sailed through the air.

Reed grabbed Monica's arm and whisked her into his building's entryway. He pressed her up against the brick wall, sheltering her with his body, as the club landed with a crash. Both of them breathing rapidly, she could feel the warmth of his breath against her face, their hearts thumping in unison. She stared up into his blue eyes, almost forgetting that the club had probably just gone through her office window.

"My car," Albert sputtered in disbelief.

"Shit." Reed rolled his eyes, stepping back away from her.

Monica bolted out onto the sidewalk, her gaze darting over to a gray Volvo with a golf club protruding from the windshield.

Marjorie glanced over at Albert, looking mortified. "I'm so sorry."

"What about me?" her husband demanded, walking over to Albert's car. He carefully maneuvered the bent club from the windshield. "I bought this at St. Andrews in Scotland. It cost over five hundred bucks." He glanced over at Reed. "Make sure that comes out of her settlement."

The woman scowled. "It might be bent but I can still stick it up your . . . "

While the two went at it, Monica glared at Reed. "See, *that's* why you're bad for business. Look at the type of clients you attract." She pointed at Albert's car.

Reed held up his hands in defense. "She's not even my client."

"So, she's here *because* of your client. I knew this would happen. It was inevitable." A sharp pain pierced her chest and she sucked in some air, unable to breath.

Her second panic attack!

She squeezed her eyes shut, hand to her chest, and softly started singing "Love and Marriage" from her Sinatra CD. "Love and Marriage," she sucked in a ragged breath and exhaled, "Love and—"

"You okay?" Reed asked. "Can I do something?"

Her eyes shot open. "Yeah, you can move."

*

Marjorie wrote Albert a check on the spot. Without waiting for the windshield to be replaced, Albert raced off, grumbling about his wife not letting him go on some golf trip. He practically left skid marks in front of Monica's office, without leaving the down payment for his balloon ride. She was now down to two clients, since that was undoubtedly the last she'd seen of Albert. Wish she could say the same for Reed Walker.

Thanks to her good riddance spell, he'd be gone before long.

Late that afternoon, Jordan helped Monica slide a baby lilac bush in a large terracotta pot to the edge of the bed of Jordan's boyfriend's truck. They hoisted it off, then trudged over to the sidewalk and set it down between her and Reed Walker's offices. Jordan claimed lilacs warded off evil. Buried in the soil were several green obsidian stones, protecting Monica from difficult people. The cloves sprinkled over the dirt were to zap negative energy.

Reed Walker was history.

Monica closed her eyes, inhaling the scent of the purple blooms, then slowly exhaled. "By wind and flame, stone and sea, keep evil forces, away from me. Be gone," she said, sprinkling patchouli oil over the bush.

"What are you doing?" Reed asked behind her.

Monica jumped, spilling the vial of patchouli oil down the front of her blouse. Lovely. "Look what you did." She pointed at the stain on her left breast.

Reed eyed her breast.

"Stop staring," she said, trying to sound offended rather than turned on.

An incredulous look consumed his face. "You *told* me to look."

"At the *stain*."

He shook his head in frustration. "I keep getting blamed for a lot things I don't do." He glanced over at Jordan and introduced himself.

"Nice to meet you." Jordan's posture went ramrod straight, her shoulders back, breasts thrust out at attention.

Good grief. Monica shot her a look that said *Hel-lo, it's not nice to meet him*, reminding her of the purpose of the lilac bush and the spell.

Reed gestured toward the bush. "Looks nice. Adds some curb appeal."

"It does, doesn't it?" Jordan said proudly.

He peered down at the bush again. "Guess I'm not the only one who likes it."

Monica glanced over at a beagle lifting its hind leg, peeing in the terracotta pot. "Get away!" she yelled, waving her arms around wildly.

The dog gazed up at her with somber brown eyes, then slowly lowered its leg and trotted off.

Monica groaned, glaring at the puddle in the soil.

"It'll be fine. Won't kill it." Reed smiled reassuringly.

"Will it kill the spell?" she asked Jordan in a panic.

Reed raised a skeptical brow. "Spell?"

"It's for attracting positive energy," Jordan said.

"And repelling *negative* energy," Monica added, eying Reed.

Jordan explained about the cosmic forces in the universe, karma, and all that jazz. Reed stared at her like she'd just landed her saucer, asking for directions to Mars.

"Not like it's black magic," Jordan said defensively, no longer sticking out her breasts.

Reed looked a tad freaked out, so Monica played it up for all it was worth. "No, *that's* not," she said, gesturing to the lilac bush, "but the doll in my office is. So if your skin starts feeling a little prickly," she poked the air with an imaginary pin, "you know what it is."

Reed's lips curled into a smirk. "That would certainly explain the *pain* I'm feeling in my ass lately." He turned and walked inside. She eyed his butt hidden beneath the suit jacket. A mighty *fine* ass no doubt.

"A voodoo doll?" Jordan said, smacking Monica in the arm. "Don't go spreading rumors like that. I'm a respectable psychic, not some carnival sideshow. I have a reputation here."

"Whatever it takes to get rid of this guy." She sprinkled more patchouli oil over the lilac bush, finally dumping the entire bottle on it for good measure. "That should do it."

A blond woman in a white linen dress walked up to Monica's office, preparing to head inside.

"Can I help you?" Monica asked.

The woman turned toward her. "Are you Monica Jackson?"

Monica nodded. "Yeah."

"I'm Megan Sullivan with the *Milwaukee Post*. I was wondering if I could to talk to you about writing an article on your business."

"An article? Ah, yeah, of course, that'd be great. How'd you hear about my company? Did you see the engagement proposal at the Brewers game last weekend?"

Megan smiled hesitantly, glancing around. "Actually I was driving by the other day and saw your place."

Monica peered over at the lilac bush. Talk about quick. It was already bringing more positive energy into her life.

The city was about to have a run on patchouli oil.

Chapter Four

Reed's mother still lived in the same house he'd grown up in, located in a middle-class suburb of Milwaukee, comprised of small ranch houses with unattached garages containing Fords and Chevys. The modest sized lawns were immaculately groomed and concrete patios held grills and lawn furniture, inviting neighbors to pop over for a beer.

God he wished she would move.

Two years ago, he'd surprised her with a brick English Tudor house in an affluent neighborhood just north of the city, a mile from his house. She'd refused to move, saying her house held too many memories. Memories Reed preferred to forget. He couldn't believe she didn't feel the same way.

"This beef is good," he said, glancing over at his mother, sitting across the patio table from him. She had on khakis and a jean shirt with embroidered bumblebees. A straw hat covered her silver hair. She'd obviously spent the afternoon tending to her flowerbeds and vegetable garden.

She set down her knife, her blue eyes filling with suspicion. "That's the third time you've said that. You're obviously buttering me up for something. Let's have it."

If it weren't for the media frenzy that was likely to ensue next week when the city's highest profile divorce ever was made public, he wouldn't bother mentioning his involvement in it.

"I'm representing Natalie Bartolli in her divorce." He sounded matter-of-fact. The topic wasn't open for discussion.

Her expression was a mix of disappointment and concern. Like the time he'd beat the crap out of Bobby Fender, who'd teased him for wearing his old snow boots, which Reed's mother had bought at the Fender's rummage sale. "Reed, let it go."

"She's a paying client like any other and needs my help."

"You have plenty of paying clients."

But he'd waited twenty-one years for his *father* to pay.

And now, he was going to pay big time. Although Reed's stepmom had offered him a percentage of her settlement in addition to his fee, he didn't want the bastard's money. He'd proven he could do just fine without it. But he wanted to ensure Natalie got a fair settlement. When Natalie married his father, she hadn't known about Reed and his mother. She'd found out several years later when Reed was in his early twenties and ran into them at a restaurant. Reed went ballistic and the manager had escorted him out. She'd contacted Reed shortly after, wanting to talk, but he'd made it clear he wanted nothing to do with them. Then two days ago, she'd walked back into his life, asking him to represent her. He'd have taken her case on pro-bono for the opportunity to destroy his father.

"I'm going to make sure he doesn't screw his second wife out of a fair settlement like he did us. I'd think that'd make you happy."

"I've let go of the past. Wish you would." Her eyes pleaded with him and he glanced away, staring into his wineglass. "This has been eating away at you for too many years."

How the hell wasn't it eating away at her? She'd worked two jobs to support them, and Reed had worked at his Uncle Marco's restaurant since he was ten. She used to drive their rusted-out car across town to grocery shop because she didn't want the neighbors knowing she used food stamps. Besides buying their clothes at rummage sales, Reed's Christmas toys came from donations through the toy drive. Not only had his father taken what money should have been theirs, he'd taken their self-respect.

Now it was Reed's turn to take away his father's.

"I didn't tell you this so you could talk me out of it. Just wanted you to know before you heard it on the news or read about it in the paper."

"You never want people to know he's your father. His divorce will attract a lot of media attention and it's bound to come out that you took my maiden name."

He knew she only wanted what she thought was best for him, but in this case, she was dead wrong. Reed glanced around at the ceramic pots on the patio, overflowing with purple, pink, and yellow flowers and vines. "Flowers are looking good."

"Changing the subject isn't going to change how I feel about this." She reached over and plucked a dried up petunia from the pot on the center of the table. "Are you coming over for dinner Sunday? I've invited Bill. I'm making pot roast."

Reed's favorite. Now who was doing the sucking up? "I'll try to make it."

Her soft, slightly rounded features hardened. "We're engaged," she said firmly. "I'd like it if you could at least have dinner together."

"And I'd like it if you agreed to do a prenup, Mom." He failed at keeping the frustration out of his voice.

Upon starting his first job, he'd opened her a retirement account and had stuck away money every paycheck. She'd accumulated a hefty sum and he wasn't about to see her lose it. Bill's track record sucked. Having been divorced four times, he didn't exactly have staying power. His last divorce had been to a fairly wealthy woman and he'd made out in spades. When Reed had questioned his mother about Bill's previous wives, she'd only known about one, his second. Reed hadn't mentioned the other three since he'd become privy to them thanks to the private investigator he'd hired to do a background check on this guy. His mother would go postal if she discovered Reed had done this.

"Take your money back," she said, dropping her knife on her plate with a clank. "I don't want it."

"I'm not taking it back," he said calmly. "It's yours."

"If it's mine, then I should be able to do what I want with it. That money doesn't make me happy—Bill does. My generation didn't do prenups. They just weren't done and I still don't think they should be. It's not right. That's not what marriage is about."

Even after everything with his father, and several failed relationships, she still thought with her heart rather than her head. She let her emotions dictate her actions. The times he'd gotten to know his mother's boyfriends, they'd never stuck around. Hopefully Bill would be different, but better to be cautious than broke.

"You know how that makes me feel, that you're so sure he's going to leave me? Like I'm not worth staying around for." The anger and frustration faded from her face and voice, and hurt filled her eyes.

Oh Christ. Was it so difficult for a woman to have a serious conversation without becoming all emotional? Making his mother cry would be the cherry on his day. "No man in his right mind would leave you. It has nothing to do with you. I just want you to be happy."

"I am." The corners of her mouth slowly curled into a smile and she reached across the table and gave his hand a loving squeeze. "You'll like Bill once you get to know him."

Reed nodded faintly. Even if his mother refused to do a prenup, he'd make sure Bill didn't get a dime, since he'd likely kill the guy for hurting his mother.

Chapter Five

Monica arrived home that night, psyched about her interview with the reporter. The article running on the front page of tomorrow's Lifestyle section would be better exposure than any event she could plan.

She slid her briefcase off her shoulder and let it drop to the floor with a thud. She glared at it. Her celebratory mood was dampened by the fact that she had to compile a monthly financial statement, including last month's. Not fun.

She grabbed the mail from the wire basket on the table by the door. Three bills and an announcement for her sister Gretchen, who was graduating with her PhD in psychology in two weeks. Overachiever. When they were growing up, Gretchen used to spend all her time studying, while Monica organized neighborhood carnivals and theater productions in their back yard. Monica and Hope had more in common than she and Gretchen. She tossed the envelope back in the basket.

"Oh hi," Hope said, walking out of the kitchen, wearing a bright smile and a white apron that read *Baking Is a Piece of Cake.* The apron, Hope, and the large knife in her hand, were covered in yellow cake and white frosting. She plucked a glob from her cheek and stuck it in her mouth.

"How's it going?" Monica asked cautiously.

"Super. I'm feeling much better."

Monica glanced in the dining room at the remains of a mutilated wedding cake strewn across the table.

"The couple just called off their wedding tomorrow," Hope said. "Better she found out he's a total ass now than after the wedding."

Hope really needed to consider a career change. At least until her divorce was final.

"Wanna see what I did today?"

Monica eyed the cake. Wasn't it obvious?

Hope grasped hold of Monica's hand, squeezing frosting between Monica's fingers. She whisked her up the stairs to Monica's bedroom.

"Ta-da!" Hope swept an arm through the air in front of the closet. It was filled with hanging rods, shelves, drawers, and wire bins. Her shirts, skirts, dresses, and pants hung neatly in separate sections.

What a freakin' nightmare.

"Hanging your clothes at varying heights allows you to maximize the space. I put casual shirts in this section and dressier ones over here. They're sorted darkest to lightest." She gestured toward a stack of three small wire bins with open fronts. "You can sort your clothes by darks, brights, and whites right when you take them off. Isn't it great?"

Monica was lucky if she sorted her clothes before throwing them in the washing machine. And the baskets were puny, overflowing with dirty clothes. She could fit a few days' worth of undies and tees in there at best. What was she supposed to do with two to three weeks' worth of laundry?

"No more shoes strewn across the closet floor. They go in these little cubbies."

Whenever Monica walked through the bedroom door, she flung the shoe off her foot and it sailed across the room right into the closet. It had taken her weeks to perfect her aim. It would take her years to get a shoe to land in one of those little square slots.

"But this is the best," Hope squealed, opening a drawer. "A drawer cubicle."

Monica's bras and undies were folded and lined up in an orderly fashion, according to color, in clear plastic trays.

What kind of sick person *folded* their underwear?

Monica took a few calming breaths, not wanting to bring on another panic attack. Her life could be worse. She could be married to Kyle. Who was the woman on the edge here, her or Hope?

Monica plastered on a smile. "This is great. Thanks." Hope obviously had too much time on her hands. "Would you have time to help me do a financial statement?"

Besides being a part-time cake decorator, until last week, Hope had done the books for her and Kyle's restaurant, K & H Steakhouse. Hope had worked out of her home—since it was kind of hard for Kyle to boff the waitresses with his wife around. And Kyle had never wanted her working full-time so she could take care of their home. Although the only child they had was Kyle.

Hope smiled wide. "Absolutely. That'd be fun."

Yeah, right up there with sponge painting the entire townhouse or preparing a Thanksgiving dinner with the fixings.

Two hours later, Monica was sitting at the desk in her bedroom, working on a proposal, when Hope rapped on the door and walked in. She'd showered off the cake and frosting and had exchanged her apron for a pink floral sundress.

"Do you plan on paying Jordan next Friday with an IOU?" Hope gazed at Monica over the top of black rectangular glasses.

"She's a volunteer. She doesn't get paid."

"Still, look at your cash flow statement." Hope placed the report on the desk in front of Monica and pointed at the bottom line, which showed a negative number. Monica's eyes widened in disbelief. "If you don't do something quick, you're gonna have a negative cash balance at the end of the month. That's only seventeen days away."

Monica's gaze narrowed. "How'd that happen?"

"I didn't figure in any expected cash sales or receivable collections, since I can't count on you to collect from clients. Like this dude who proposed at the Brewers game last Sunday. The event is over, and he's only paid half his bill."

"The ring ended up costing more than he'd thought. It was gorgeous with a platinum . . . "

"It's not your responsibility to finance his ring."

A week ago, Hope would have been all about the ring.

"You have to have cash flowing in before it can flow out. There are three ways to increase profit. By increasing your sales or prices, or decreasing expenses."

Monica smiled. "Sales are gonna be booming." She told Hope about the article in the paper.

Hope's professional demeanor vanished and she threw her arms around Monica, giving her a huge hug. "Yay! Looks like your career spell's working."

The portable phone rang out on the nightstand. Kyle and Hope's number displayed on the caller ID.

"Should I answer it?" Monica asked cautiously.

Hope nodded, nibbling nervously on her lower lip. She claimed she hadn't spoken to Kyle since she'd caught him in the act and muttered, "Those are our new sheets." Monica, on the other hand, enjoyed her little chats with Kyle. They were becoming the highlight of her day. Which didn't take much lately.

Monica hit the speakerphone button. "Hello," she said sweetly.

"Where the hell's Hope?" Kyle's voice blared from the speaker.

"I have no clue," Monica said innocently, then flashed Hope a mischievous grin.

"Doesn't matter, I'm sure you had something to do with my Rolex. Been looking for it since Hope left. You sure as hell better not have sold it."

What was with blaming Monica for everything? Granted, she wanted to advise Hope to sell the watch rather than to bury it, but she hadn't.

"Oh, we didn't *sell* it. We used it in the spell we cast to warn all women you're a total dirtbag and to stay away from you." Maybe it was about time to start giving Hope some credit so Kyle realized she was no longer a meek little housewife willing to forgive him for a new pair of cotton sheets.

"A spell? Are you off your friggin' rocker? What kind of a stupid-ass idea is that?"

"I heard your skank girlfriend got back with her hubby," Hope blurted out in the background. "Guess the spell's working. Not such a stupid ass idea, hey?"

"I knew you were there, Hope. If I don't have my Rolex back in twenty-four hours I'm calling the police." Click. Dead air.

Monica hit the speakerphone button, turning it off.

Hope collapsed down on the desk chair, blowing out a huff of air, her shoulders dropping. "Holy crap. Can't believe I just talked to him." She glanced over at Monica. "Looks like your career spell isn't the only one working. Going over to my house every night and chanting over the buried sock seems to be paying off." A possessed look filled her eyes and consumed her face. "Moonlight, glowing bright, warn all . . . "

"Stop chanting," Monica commanded, heart racing. "I think *that* spell is bringing me *bad* luck." She told Hope about Reed Walker and the sign. *Marriage isn't a word, it's a sentence. I'll set you free.*

Rather than rallying to support Monica, Hope laughed. "That's classic. Think I'll have it made into a bumper sticker." She whisked out of the room.

Monica let out a frustrated groan, dropping back in her chair. Once Reed was gone, Hope and her negative energy were next on her list.

Chapter Six

A Saturday morning, and instead of being at Jordan's cookout or at the Renaissance Faire for fun, Monica was at the Faire working an event. She shouldn't whine. One of her college friends worked every weekend for the past three years and it had landed her a lucrative sales director position at an upscale hotel in San Francisco. This friend would give her right kidney if it meant landing a medical account. Monica wasn't willing to donate her internal organs, but she could give up her weekends, since that was when most of her events took place.

She was much better prepared for this event than the previous six she'd done. The violinist had no-showed on the last one, so she now had a backup barmaid on alert to serve goblets of champagne, since she hadn't yet seen Sissy, her original hire. She'd rehearsed the proposal with her client Jeff until they both knew it by heart, so he wouldn't have a Freudian slip and ask his girlfriend to *bury* him rather than *marry* him, which had happened at engagement proposal number two. And even though there wasn't a cloud in sight, Monica had scouted out a nearby tent they could duck under if the sky suddenly opened up and poured on them. This job was seriously making her a pessimist.

Located in a remote area of the grounds, the Nobles Glen was serenely romantic. At the front, lush ivy blanketed a massive stone wall, and garlands of yellow flowers trailed across the top. Grecian urns overflowed with pink and purple petunias, and pristine statues of angels and cherubs were poised throughout. Everything was perfect.

Almost *too* perfect.

Shortly after she arrived in the glen, Jeff came running up, glancing over his shoulder. "I had a hard time ditching Trish without her getting suspicious." He raked a nervous hand through his blond hair, letting out a heavy sigh and the stench of ale.

It was only ten in the morning for crying out loud, and he was way too skinny to hold his booze. He'd be gassed by the time he proposed. He wiped perspiration from his forehead, sweating bullets, yet his face was a pasty white.

Monica gave him a reassuring smile. "Everyone gets nervous before they propose. Asking someone to marry you is a big step. Why would you have gone to all this trouble planning such a romantic proposal if you didn't really love her?"

"I just feel really . . . " He gazed past Monica, over at the girl approaching.

It was Sissy, the barmaid who'd be serving the champagne. Her breasts—beaded with perspiration—were spilling out of her gauze chemise, thanks to the tightly laced bodice.

Monica introduced them.

Jeff smiled wide, ogling Sissy's breasts.

"Here's the necklace." Monica handed him a chain with a medallion. "Do you remember what you're supposed to say when you put it on her?"

Jeff's forehead scrunched as he searched for an answer.

"Maybe you should practice."

"Yeah, maybe." He turned to Sissy and placed the chain around her neck. "Here's an Angelic Moose—"

"Muse," Monica corrected. Oh man, not another Freudian slip.

"Right." He stared at the medallion nestled between Sissy's breasts.

"How sweet," Sissy said, pressing a hand against the medallion, molding it to her breasts.

The color was back in Jeff's face and a bright red.

Unbelievable.

Monica held out her hand. Sissy removed the necklace and dropped it in Monica's palm. Monica handed it to Jeff. "After you put the necklace on Trish, the minstrel will stroll out from behind the stone wall playing a ballad. This is your cue to propose. When the song ends, the queen will present the ring and bless your engagement. Then Sissy serves the champagne."

He smiled at Sissy.

"You better get back to Trish," Monica said, nudging him.

Jeff blinked, returning to the twenty-first century, then took off in search of his future fiancée.

A half-hour later, Sissy, Queen Elizabeth, and the minstrel were posted behind the stone wall. After Monica hiked up the neckline on Sissy's gauze chemise, she sat on a bench off to the side, reading a book, blending into the background. Jeff and Trish strolled into the glen. No longer merely pale, he looked like he was going to need a defibrillator at any moment.

He dug around in his front pants' pocket, eventually producing the medallion. He fumbled with the clasp. Trish assisted, securing the medallion around her neck. The minstrel strolled out from behind the wall, serenading them. Trish's eyes widened. The queen paraded out, dressed in an elaborate purple and gold gown, followed by Sissy in her bar wench garb.

Jeff's gaze locked on Sissy.

The queen blessed the ring, presenting it to Jeff on a purple velvet pillow. Jeff stood frozen. The queen nudged him.

He picked up the ring and paused just shy of sliding it on Trish's finger. "I can't do this," he blurted out. He glanced over at Monica. "You were right. I don't know why I went to all this trouble if I don't love her."

Talk about twisting her words.

"What!" Trish shrieked, glaring at Monica.

Jeff's gaze darted from Sissy to Trish. "I'm sorry. I'm not ready to get married."

Trish gave Monica the evil eye. "This is your fault! Telling him he shouldn't marry me!"

Monica's jaw dropped. "I never said that."

"And traipsing this slut in front of him. I'm . . . I'm suing!" Trish stormed out of the glen.

Suing? She couldn't sue Monica because her boyfriend was a sleaze bag. Could she?

This was the *only* thing Monica hadn't foreseen going wrong. A sharp pain pierced her chest and she flinched, sucking in some serious air. Breathe in, breathe out. Breathe in, breathe out.

Breathe at all!

*

"This woman can't sue you because her boyfriend's a total scum," Hope said on the other end of the phone. "She can't even sue him. If that were grounds for suing, most of the male population would be financially, as well as emotionally, bankrupt. If she wants to sue anyone, she should sue Walt Disney."

"I think he's dead," Monica said.

"She could sue his estate. He produced all those fantasy movies like *Cinderella* and *Snow White.* We were barely able to eat solid food and we were having the delusion of Prince Charming crammed down our throats. Get real, what guy is going to haul his cookies around town with a shoe looking for the perfect fit? They never did a sequel to any of those movies because they wouldn't have happy endings. The week after Cinderella got married her prince was probably sleeping with one of her butt-ugly stepsisters and—"

"You're right. I've got another call coming in," Monica lied. "Talk to you later." She snapped her phone shut.

Hope was probably right. However, people had sued for more bizarre things and won. Like that guy who stole a car, got in an accident, and was injured due to a faulty seat belt. He sued the car's owner and won. As Monica neared her office, she spotted a guy in a white T-shirt and jeans standing outside it. She zoned in on his butt, which looked incredible in a pair of Levis. She approached, realizing it was Reed standing there with a cloth, wiping something off her window. The jeans relaxed against his butt. A nice change from his black suit pants, which warned *Hands off, I've got a stick up my ass.*

Her gaze meandered from his tush up to his back muscles flexing beneath his T-shirt, then on to his biceps, as he wiped down the window. She admired the view a moment longer before glancing at the window and read what appeared to be written in blood red lipstick. *VE STINKS.* Likely the remnants of *LOVE STINKS,* courtesy of another one of his disgruntled clients no doubt.

Reed peered over at her, looking surprised to see her. "Your sign says you're closed weekends." Stubble covered his jaw and cheeks, adding to his more laid-back look. And here Monica had assumed he shaved twice daily.

"Most of my events take place on weekends, but my office is never totally closed."

The corners of his mouth curled into a smile. "I hear ya. I was open this morning and just came back to catch up on administrative crap. My assistant's on vacation. I'd get a temp, but don't have time to train someone or deal with all the screw-ups. I'm better off flying solo for two weeks."

Monica nodded. Thank God she had Jordan to keep her organized.

He gestured toward the lipstick on the window. "I swear it's not my shade."

She couldn't help but smile.

"Thought it probably wasn't good for your business."

Guess she couldn't prove it had been one of his clients, and it was really sweet of him to wipe it off after she'd threatened to poke pins in him, or at least in his voodoo doll. Besides, at the moment, somebody defacing her window was minor compared to being sued. Actually, Reed probably knew a thing or two about being sued. Vengeful spouses suing for custody of children, pets, and espresso makers were undoubtedly the norm.

"I'm being sued," she blurted out. "It wasn't my fault. I swear I never told the guy he didn't love her."

"I'm sure you wouldn't have." His eyes didn't hold the least bit of doubt. She appreciated the reassurance.

"I thought he really did love her, so why would I have said he didn't?" Sounding on the verge of hysteria, her body kicked into full panic mode, heart racing, hands sweating, breathing labored.

Rather than looking freaked out by her emotional meltdown, Reed gently grasped hold of her elbow. "Let's go inside." He led her into his office.

"That's right, I wouldn't have. I mean, I just asked him why he would go to all the trouble of planning such an elaborate proposal if he didn't truly love his girlfriend . . . " Her eyes widened and she gazed desperately at him, grasping hold of the T-shirt across his chest, clinging to it. "Omigod. That wasn't telling him he doesn't love her, was it?"

*

Attempting to calm her down, Reed placed his hands on her shoulders, gazing into her brown eyes, noticing the small flecks of green in them. She had great eyes. "No, that sure as hell isn't telling him he doesn't love her."

She nodded faintly, looking far from convinced. "What if she sues me and I lose my business? I can't lose another business. I can't lose the money everyone borrowed me. I'll be working temp jobs the rest of my life. If only I hadn't said that."

"She doesn't have—"

"What was I thinking? What if . . . " she rambled on frantically.

He gave her shoulders a little shake, but she wouldn't snap out of it. Cheeks flushed, the corners of her mouth twitching, she looked like she was about to start crying. He didn't do well with emotional women even though he dealt with them on a daily basis. He found it easiest when he turned them from weepy, hurt women into empowered, angry women. Anger was a much easier emotion to deal with. However, he didn't want Monica to be angry.

So he did the first thing he could think of to get her mind off the subject and prevent her from having a breakdown: He kissed her. The kiss, a gentle brushing of his lips against hers, was intended to be a brief diversion, until she responded by throwing her arms around his neck and kissing him back. So he went for it, deepening the kiss, slipping his tongue inside her mouth. She pressed her body against him and the fullness of her breasts caused him to instantly go hard. He slid his hands down over the curves of her ass, then back up to her waist.

He wrapped an arm around her waist and slid the other up her slender stomach. He cupped her full breast, massaging it. It felt incredible. Soft. *Real.* Unlike those of many women he dated. Her hands swept up the back of his neck and she tunneled her fingers through his hair, massaging his scalp. Her lips strayed from his, trailing kisses down his chin and across his jaw line, flicking her tongue against the thin scar marring his skin. Her kisses continued up to his earlobe, driving him insane.

He slid his hand down over her shirt and started to slip it under when she backed up against the desk. Hunger filled her eyes, yet he was unsure if she wanted him to stop, until she hooked her fingers through his front belt loops and pulled him to her. He slid his hands around to the back of her thighs and lifted her onto the desk. She spread her legs apart, her skirt hiking up her thighs. He massaged a hand along her inner thigh, stroking it, then slipped it under her skirt. He brushed his fingertips over the front of her lace thong, then along the elastic band at her leg, tempted to slide a finger beneath it.

She let out a soft moan, dropping her head back in submission. Her cheeks were flushed, lips swollen from kissing, and her entire body screamed *take me*. His office was closed, so it wasn't like any clients would wander in and catch them. But she deserved more respect than a quick screw on his desk. And he couldn't take advantage of her in her current frame of mind.

Wanting her more than any woman, it took every ounce of self-control he had, but he managed to step back.

She lifted her head up, meeting his gaze. The lustful haze in her eyes disappeared, replaced with confusion, then hurt.

He wanted to reach out and brush a finger over her swollen lips, but there was no way he'd stop there. "I'd have no regrets, but I think you would."

Rather than telling him he was way off base as he'd hoped, she slid off the desk, then yanked down her skirt.

Shit. He should have kept his mouth shut.

"This woman doesn't have a case," he said, trying to focus on something other than the sweet taste of her skin still on his lips and the lace thong under her skirt. "With all the people who back out on getting married, that'd be a much more lucrative practice for me. So forget about this and go plan another engagement proposal for a couple that *will* stay together forever."

Skepticism replaced the hurt in her eyes. "What about the fifty percent of marriages that end in divorce?"

"There's the other fifty percent that don't."

Where the hell had that come from?

Her eyes widened. "Kind of optimistic, aren't you?"

He hated seeing her so damn pessimistic. He barely knew her, but he knew it wasn't her nature. Besides, he was used to telling people whatever made them feel better. As long as he said something with confidence, people believed anything.

"Did you see your article in this morning's paper?" he asked, changing the subject, gesturing toward the newspaper on the edge of his desk, opened to the article on her business.

Smiling, she grabbed the paper and studied the photo. "That picture turned out great." The photo was of her standing proudly in front of her office, taken from a strategic angle likely intended to exclude his office. "This is just what my business needs."

Yes, it was. Megan Sullivan had owed him one. Now, they were even. He'd felt bad over the golf club incident yesterday, even though it hadn't directly been his fault. Monica was obviously struggling to keep her business afloat and couldn't afford to lose any clients. Like a marriage, a small business only had a fifty percent shot at succeeding. He'd been one of the lucky ones. But he'd seen a lot of businesses fold due to failed marriages. Women often couldn't handle the financial or emotional stress of running a family-owned business without their husbands. He didn't want to see Monica's business fail.

If she'd known he'd arranged for the article, she'd either have refused help from the enemy or read more into it than there was. No matter how attracted he was to her, they would always be on opposing sides. She wanted some fairytale romance. A man who bought her flowers and surprised her with romantic candlelit dinners. One who would put her before work. Who would stay the night. She'd expect all kinds of things he wouldn't be able to give her and she deserved.

He needed a woman without expectations.

Chapter Seven

Monica unlocked the front door of her office, Reed's newspaper still in hand. She wasn't sure if it was the article or having been mere minutes from an orgasm that had put the spring in her step. If Reed hadn't stopped, she wouldn't have. And he was right, she'd have regretted it. Having sex on Reed's desk would hardly convince him she wanted him gone. Yet, it bugged her that he'd stopped. What was that about? He was constantly staring at her breasts and he'd kissed her first.

She walked inside and her nose crinkled. The stench of Chico's enchilada special from yesterday clung to the hundred-percent humidity hovering in the air. Eeewww. She came to an abrupt halt, slapping a hand over her mouth. Since it was at least twenty degrees cooler outside, she propped the door open with a chair.

What happened to the air conditioning?

Jordan was off, or she'd have been on top of it. Monica called and left a message for her landlord. Being Saturday, he probably wouldn't return her call immediately, so she phoned Hope and asked her to bring over some fans. Then she saturated the stale air with lavender disinfectant spray.

She decided to work on something that didn't require a lot of concentration, so she started slapping the red heart transparencies she'd bought last week on the front window. She had to do something to compete with Reed's sign. After the window was framed in hearts, she went into her office and tried to focus on planning an engagement proposal for the upcoming Italian fest. Being Italian, she was in her element and her brain flooded with ideas.

An hour later, she finally decided on a gondola ride down the Milwaukee River, with a gondolier serenading the couple as they passed under the Wells Street Bridge and a banner dropped down that read *Will You Marry Me—Insert Name?*

Perfect. Now she just needed a client to plan it for.

She wiped the perspiration from her forehead. Where was Hope with the fans?

She walked out to the hallway leading back to the bathroom and opened the dorm-sized fridge that was still humming. Fanning herself with the door did little to cool her off. She plucked a small ice cube from a tray. She swept it down her neck, beneath her white wrap shirt, and tucked it inside her bra. Ahh . . . she slipped an ice cube in the other cup. A minute should do the trick. She rubbed an ice cube across her forehead, down her cheeks, then her neck, making her skin slick with water.

"Excuse me," a man called out.

The ice cube went flying from her fingertips, landing on the carpet. "As Time Goes By" hadn't signaled his arrival since the door was propped open. She poked her head around the corner. Luckily, it was the mailman rather than a client. She told him to set the mail on the desk while she grabbed a towel and wiped the moisture off her face. She walked over to Jordan's desk, where the headline on one of the newly delivered magazines caught her eye: *How to Cure a Divorce Hangover*. A divorce magazine? What if a client had seen this? On top of the magazine were several pieces of mail addressed to Reed Walker's law firm, but with her address. He'd given out her address by mistake? Lovely.

She couldn't believe she'd kissed that man.

Magazine clenched in hand, she marched out of the office and next door to Reed's. A blast of cool air greeted her, stopping her dead in her tracks. She wiped perspiration from her forehead, then continued past the receptionist's desk. Reed's office door was cracked open and the sound of Hope's sobbing voice carried into the outer office. Was Reed making her cry?

Monica was about to storm in when Hope wailed, "How could I have been so stupid?"

Monica flattened herself against the wall, listening.

"Trusting someone isn't being stupid," Reed said. "Kyle was stupid for breaking your trust. Hell, Kyle was stupid for a lot of reasons."

Amen. Kyle was just plain stupid.

"I feel like a failure," Hope said, sniffling.

"Why? You made a vow to Kyle and you kept it. Kyle failed. He'll continue to fail, while you succeed."

"I will?" This was the first hint of optimism Monica had heard in Hope's voice in over a week, even though Monica had tried to convince her she was better off without the loser.

"Of course you will. You can accomplish whatever you set your mind to. There's nothing you can't do."

"You're right," Hope said, sounding inspired. "I'm not a failure. I'm going to start a new life. A better one."

Reed Walker—Grief Therapist and Motivational Speaker?

More like cutthroat lawyer who said whatever it took to land a client.

Omigod. Did Hope plan to hire Reed?

Monica flew into the office without knocking.

There sat Hope, two fans at her feet, dabbing tears from her cheeks with a tissue. She glanced over at Monica and plastered on one of her perky smiles. "Sorry, I got sidetracked. I just hired Reed to represent me. He represented my friends Roberta and Ashley and they made a haul. He's the best divorce lawyer in the city. I didn't know Reed was the lawyer next to you."

Was Monica the only woman in Milwaukee who hadn't heard of Reed Walker, divorce lawyer extraordinaire, a.k.a. one of the city's most eligible bachelors? After she'd taken Hope in, how could she turn around and betray her like this? Not that she didn't want Hope to have a good lawyer, but she didn't want to give Reed business. They would discuss this later when Monica wasn't on the verge of heatstroke.

Hope stood and shook Reed's hand. "Thanks for seeing me when you weren't even open. I'll be in touch." She grabbed the fans. "I'll drop these in your office." She breezed out, looking like a new woman, like she'd just spent the week at a spa or had run Kyle down with her car.

Monica tossed Reed's mail on the desk, her gaze zoning in on the area where she'd been sitting earlier with him between her legs. She recalled the feel of his hand skimming up her thigh, beneath her skirt, his light touch teasing her thong . . .

She wiped perspiration from behind her neck. "I'd appreciate it if you informed the mailman of your correct address." She peered up from the desk to find his intense gaze caressing her breasts like his hands had done earlier. Her entire body went even warmer. Did he want to pick up where they'd left off? Did he regret pushing her away?

Monica peered down at her white shirt clinging to the outline of her sheer white bra, both of them wet from the melted ice cubes. Her nipples stood erect from the cool air and Reed's stare. She tried not to look mortified. He probably thought she kept intentionally doing things to draw attention to her breasts. Was she making Freudian slip-ups? Did she want to seduce this guy?

Of course not. She snatched up the divorce magazine and held it in front of her. "My air conditioning's on the fritz."

Reed glanced down at his desk, straightening a pile of orderly files. "Oh man, no air, that sucks."

Whoa. Mr. Unflappable was stuttering like a teenage virgin at a wet T-shirt contest. For once, she was more in control than Reed. Knowing that would be short-lived, and they would end up back on his desk if she remained there, she tossed the magazine on the desk, turned around, and bolted out.

*

Monica snagged the vial of patchouli oil from her desk drawer and marched out to the lilac bush, even more determined to get rid of Reed. She dumped the entire bottle over the top of the bush and watched the oil slither down over the blooms and branches, leaving a glossy sheen in its wake, some of it eventually forming quivering droplets on the soil. She really needed to ration out the expensive oil at least over the course of a day, or switch to a spray. Maybe she could stick patchouli candles in the soil and let them burn all day long. She'd have to run that by Jordan on Monday.

A few hours later, she sat at her desk, optimistically brainstorming event ideas for potential future clients. The fans were blowing at her feet so they didn't send the sticky notes and papers flying off the desk. Still no air. Amazingly, her shirt had dried in the humidity. And dealing with the heat was better than going home and confronting Hope about hiring Reed. Besides, Monica was torn. She didn't want Reed representing Hope, yet he'd made her sound so positive. Maybe he could get her to stop mutilating cakes and chanting over Kyle's sock.

Monica glanced out into the lobby, spotting a woman. She hurried out, unsure how long the woman had been standing there waiting. In her early fifties, she was tall and slender with stunning silver hair and blue eyes, which matched her long rayon sundress.

The woman glanced away from the *Casablanca* poster and over at Monica, wearing a kind smile that included her eyes. "You know Bogart never said, 'Play it again Sam,'" she said, imitating Bogie's suave manner. "He said, 'You played it for her, you can play it for me.'"

Monica smiled, nodding. "Although Ingrid Bergman did say, 'Play it, Sam.'"

The woman looked impressed. "Thought I was the only one who'd seen the movie so many times I could pick out the misquoted lines."

"I'm a classic movie junkie." Monica wiped the perspiration from her upper lip. “Sorry about the heat. The air conditioning is broke.”

The woman waved away Monica’s concern. “I’ve never had air in my house or car. Prefer to have the windows open. So few months we can do that in Wisconsin, I have to take advantage of it regardless of the heat.” She glanced over at the red upholstered chairs. “Aren’t those pretty.” She walked over and sat, relaxing back in the chair. “Comfy. I’m looking for new chairs for my living room.”

The first client to sit in the chairs. A very good sign.

“I bought them at a consignment store,” Monica admitted.

“Too bad. I’d sure like a set.” The woman pushed herself up from the chair. “So do your romantic events only include engagement proposals and anniversaries?”

“No, pretty much anything to do with romance. I did a dinner for a guy who barely even knew a girl, but wanted to woo her. Were you wanting to plan something?”

She nodded. “I want to get my son back together with his girlfriend. He’s too stubborn to admit he was wrong breaking up with her.”

“They usually are.”

The woman introduced herself as Lila and Monica led her into her office where they sat down.

“Why don’t you tell me a bit about your son and this girl so I can get a feel for what type of event might be best for them. What did they have in common?”

Lila stared at her hands folded on her lap, as if praying, like this was her last hope for her son. After pondering the question a moment she said, “He had lobster flown in from Maine for dinner once. They said it was the best ever.”

A love of lobster had been the basis for their relationship? Didn’t sound promising.

“Don’t get me wrong, they cared a lot about each other. He was always so busy he didn’t bring her around much so I never got to know her real well.”

Monica set down her pen. "If you don't mind me asking, why do you think they belong together?"

"They dated for almost *four* months." Lila sounded in awe, as if speaking of a couple celebrating their fiftieth wedding anniversary. "He's never dated a woman nearly that long. He must have cared dearly for her. She paid five thousand dollars at a charity benefit to win a date with him. Such a romantic start."

A red flag went up. Charity auction? Jordan had mentioned Reed had been auctioned off for five grand.

Lila gazed out at the movie posters in the lobby. "When he was younger we used to watch old movies together. He loved *Casablanca*. Not because it was romantic, but he liked Bogart. Thought he was a tough guy. He used to walk around the house imitating him."

Monica smiled as if to say *How adorable*, then cut to the chase. "What's your son's name?"

"Reed Walker. You probably know him. His law office is next door. I was going to see him when I saw your sign. But please don't tell him I came here," she said, lowering her voice, like he could suddenly hear her through the walls.

"Of course not. Client confidentiality."

Lila was so sweet, Monica didn't have the heart to tell her she should invest her money in something that was more likely to pay off. Like a ski resort in Palm Beach. No way was Reed ever getting married with his attitude. Yet, Lila seemed so confident that this woman was the one for him. A pang of jealousy shot through Monica. What was Reed doing kissing her if he was hot for another woman? Trying to get over her? If Reed got back with his old girlfriend, maybe Monica would stop having fantasies of the two of them on his desk.

Besides, she couldn't afford to turn away a client.

"If he likes the movie *Casablanca*, I could recreate Rick's Place, at least somewhat. I have a friend who owns a Moroccan restaurant.

It's closed on Sundays. Maybe I could use it for a private dinner." Ted owed her a favor since she'd set him up on a blind date that had led to marriage six months later.

"I don't know how you'll get him there. He doesn't eat dinner half the time. He's always at his office." A conspiratorial expression spread across Lila's face. "You could have someone call and pretend to be a prospective client wanting to meet over dinner."

Monica liked how this woman's mind worked.

Her son undoubtedly wouldn't.

Chapter Eight

Reed walked into the dimly lit Moroccan restaurant. Granted, it might not be the most popular ethnic food in Milwaukee, but the place was deserted except for a guy at a piano playing "As Time Goes By" and a woman sitting at a table with her back to him, obviously his new client. The restaurant looked like something out of Arabian Nights. Red and gold sheers tented the ceiling and a red oriental rug covered the floor. Wooden tables sat low to the ground and diners had the seating choice of short, ornately upholstered stools or overstuffed cushions. Exotic spices and garlic filled the air.

He walked toward the woman. A short white dress showed off her slender tan legs and her long blond hair was pulled back in a twist. She was hot, at least from the back. Too bad he never dated clients. Maybe some meaningless sex would help get the feel of Monica's lace thong off his mind. You'd think he was fourteen and it was the first pair of girl's panties he'd ever felt for Christ's sake.

He approached the woman and was about to say hello when she turned to him, wearing a psychotic grin that still haunted him.

Cynthia Reynolds.

What the hell? The candle flickering on the table cast a yellow glow against her face, making her eyes look even more possessed. Panic pressed against his chest, causing him to suck in some air, inhaling a lethal dose of her signature perfume, *Poison*.

"Cynthia," he muttered, his throat feeling like it was closing up. He gave his shirt collar a solid tug, loosening his tie.

She sprang from the chair, planting a kiss on his lips. He suddenly realized the music had stopped and his gaze darted over at the piano to find the guy gone. Shit. No witnesses. He couldn't believe she'd lured him to a deserted restaurant. How hadn't he recognized her voice on the phone? He peered over at a sword display on the wall, wondering what she had planned for him. He had a sick feeling it was worse than *The Walkers* website she'd created showcasing superimposed photos of their alleged wedding, kids, home, and entire friggin' life.

"How you been?" She placed a hand gently on his forearm, stroking a lethal red nail down the sleeve of his white oxford. Temporarily frozen by sheer panic, he finally regained his senses when her finger brushed against his hand. He promptly retracted his hand, not wanting her to feel the sweat on his palms and detect fear, something she got off on.

"What have you been up to?" she asked.

Nice try. This chick undoubtedly had a shrine dedicated to him, hidden away in the depths of her basement. Comprised of recent photos, articles, and newspaper clippings, along with a lock of his hair pinned to a doll in a black suit, laid out on a cement slab. She'd make any voodoo doll Monica had look like a Malibu Ken doll.

"What are you doing here?" he said calmly.

Besides violating the restraining order. After he'd broken up with her earlier that year, she'd stalked him for three months. Two months longer than they'd dated. Not having seen her in several weeks, he'd hoped she'd moved to Australia, or a rubber room. He didn't care which.

"When I found out you wanted to get back together, of course I came. I knew you'd come around."

One of the many voices in her head was obviously making her delusional again.

She once again placed a hand on his arm and his gaze darted around nervously, searching for signs of what she might have up her sleeve. He spied Monica peering at him through the window in the kitchen door. What the hell was she doing there? Had she orchestrated this entire thing? Apparently she would go to great lengths to get rid of him. Permanently.

Cynthia followed his gaze to the door where Monica stood. "Why are you staring at *her*?" she demanded. Just like that. Stable to psychotic in seconds flat. She placed a hand on his cheek, forcefully turning his head to face her. "What, you have a *thing* for her? You think she's *prettier* than me? Are you sleeping with her!" She glared at the kitchen door, a deranged look on her face. "Get out here, bitch, or I'm coming in there!"

Reed's gaze darted to the door. No Monica. She had probably high-tailed it out the back, abandoning him.

Fists at her side, Cynthia stalked toward the kitchen. Reed grabbed hold of her arm. She attempted to jerk her arm free and he tightened his grip. "If you leave right now, I won't press charges. Otherwise, I'm making your life a living hell. This is the third time you've violated the restraining order. You'll go to jail."

"Living without you has made my life a living hell!" Cynthia clamped her nails down on his arm and he yelled out in pain as they pierced his skin through his shirtsleeve. He released her arm.

Monica flew out of the kitchen, rifling through her purse. She whipped out a spray can and held it out in front of her. "Get out of here or I'll blind you for life." Cynthia took a step toward Monica and Monica pretended to press her finger down on the can. "This is your last chance."

"Fine," Cynthia snapped, practically foaming at the mouth like a rabid animal. "But this isn't over." She turned and bolted across the restaurant toward the exit.

"I meant what I said, Cynthia," he called after her. "You won't look good in an orange jumpsuit and those nails of yours will be history." He rubbed his forearm where she'd dug in her nails. The door slammed shut and he raced over and locked it.

He stormed back into the restaurant. "What the hell were you thinking? I can't believe you invited that psychotic bitch here, and back into my life." He dropped his head back and let out a frustrated growl.

Monica lowered the pepper spray, but looked like she was prepared to use it again. "I can see how dating you could make a woman lose her mind."

"Christ. Thought I was finally rid of her. This is why I don't date. A bogus paternity suit, then this psycho, what's next?"

"Gee, you poor thing. All these women want you," she said, waving her hands around wildly. He stepped back, afraid she might zap him with pepper spray either intentionally or accidentally. "I would kill for such problems. Nobody ever stalks *me*."

"Being stalked isn't a good thing."

"If somebody stalks you, it means they really like you."

"It means she's off her meds again."

Monica gazed down at the spray can in her hand, letting out a defeated sigh, her shoulders slumping. "Thirteen business plans and they've all failed. I'm not cut out to run a business. I'll be working temp jobs the rest of my life. I can't do anything right lately. This is the second event in two days that got screwed up."

Event? This had his mother written all over it. She'd been acting strange when she'd stopped by his office yesterday morning, hinting around about whether or not he was dating anyone. And no wonder she'd been fine with him blowing off dinner with her and Bill for a client meeting.

"My mother hired you, didn't she?"

She nodded faintly.

A sick feeling wrenched his gut. Monica had tried to set him up with another woman. Granted, his mother had hired her, but it still bugged the hell out of him that she'd been prepared to stand there in the kitchen and watch him have an intimate dinner with another woman. His entire body tensed at the thought of Monica at a cozy corner table in a dark restaurant with another man.

Suddenly, he could somewhat understand Cynthia's possessive behavior.

"You had no way of knowing Cynthia is a complete nutcase,"

he said reassuringly. "Even my mother didn't know. After Cynthia won a date with me at that charity auction, we dated a few times, but then she turned psycho. I never told my mother we stopped dating, so she'd lay off the fact that I didn't have a steady girlfriend."

A smile slowly curled the corners of Monica's mouth. "Your mom just wants you to be happy. She's really sweet."

She sounded slightly surprised, like she'd expected his mother to be a she-devil, having produced a son like him.

This also bugged him.

He glanced over at the table in the corner, the candle flickering across the dimly lit room. He inhaled the exotic spices filling the air. "Bet you did a great job planning the evening."

An appreciative glint filled her eyes and the defeated look on her face faded slightly. "Hope was here earlier and prepared a chicken couscous dish and a tajine. She's a phenomenal cook."

"We could eat it," he said hesitantly. "Be a shame to let it go to waste."

She twisted her mouth around, gazing down at her purple heels, looking torn. She glanced up, her gaze narrowing. "Why haven't you ever had a steady girlfriend? Hazard of the job?"

What all had she and his mother discussed? Junior prom when he'd refused to take a date over going with his buddies? Or how about the time in college when he went over a year without dating—not without sex—and his mother sat him down and tactfully asked him if he were gay, like that guy Will on TV?

He shrugged. "Suppose so."

"Maybe you just haven't found *the* one."

"Maybe."

He gazed deep into Monica's eyes, wondering what exactly he *had* found with her. His gaze traveled to her full lips with the perfect dip over the top of her mouth then down her neck to her breasts. She took a deep breath and her purple spandex top molded her breasts even tighter. He resisted the urge to reach out and massage his hands over them then down the slender curves of her waist and . . . lower. He could almost feel the texture of her lace thong against his fingertips, and the smoothness of her skin as he slid it slowly down her legs. She made a barely audible sound, a contented moan. He glanced up, their gazes locking.

Monica nibbled at her lower lip. "I, ah, should probably get going," she said, in a low, breathless tone.

He stepped forward, closing the distance between them. "I think you should stay." He wrapped his hand gently around her hand holding the can of pepper spray. "If you don't plan on using this."

She shook her head faintly, loosening her grip on the can. He slipped it from her hand and tossed it on the floor. Although, even pepper spray couldn't keep him from making love to Monica. She tossed her purse on the floor and his heart hammered against his chest, a mix of anticipation and nervousness. He couldn't recall ever having felt nervous with a woman before. His gaze followed his hands as they swept down over her full breasts, to the curves of her waist, and rested on her hips, taking it all in. Anxious to explore every inch of her body, he didn't know where to begin.

But he definitely knew how he wanted this evening to end.

*

Monica was ready to self-combust as Reed lowered his head and gently touched his lips to hers. He slid his tongue across her lower lip, then along her upper one before slipping it inside her mouth. His tongue teased the tip of hers before wrapping around it and slowly stroking it. The aroma of exotic spices and incense permeated the air, yet all she could smell was the jasmine of Reed's cologne and the musky scent of his shampoo.

She slid her hands up over his stomach muscles and fanned them across his chest—his broad, rock-solid pecs. She envisioned herself ripping off his oxford, buttons flying, her fingers clawing savagely at his chest. Probably not a good idea to come across too aggressive, or desperate, when he appeared in complete control, as usual. Damn his self-discipline.

Wanting desperately to see him lose control over *her*, she deepened the kiss, her tongue darting around his mouth with a sense of urgency. Her body melted against him, his hard erection pressing against her soft belly, her breasts molding against his chest.

He drew his head back slightly then placed a gentle kiss to her lips. "God you feel great," he muttered against her lips. "Let's not rush." He grazed the back of his fingers across her cheek.

"Okay," she said, struggling for a sliver of self-control.

His fingers curled around the bottom of her shirt, grazing her bare skin, causing her stomach to flutter and her breath to catch in her throat. She raised her arms over her head and he peeled off her shirt. He admired her fuchsia lace bra and the swells of her breasts, tracing warm feather kisses along the tops of them. He undid the clasp, then slipped his fingers under the straps, skimming them up her back, leaving goose bumps in their wake as he removed her bra.

She went to undo his tie and he grasped her hand.

"You first," he said, his voice raspy and way sexy.

His unselfish, generous attitude was completely unexpected and caused her inner thighs to throb with appreciation.

He slipped his hands around her waist and unzipped her skirt, letting it drop to her feet, leaving her standing in merely a fuchsia satin thong and purple heels. His hungry gaze traveled down over her naked body, eating it up. A hot wave of desire rippled through her, causing her cheeks to flush. She undid his purple and pink paisley tie and slid it out from beneath his shirt collar. She draped the tie around her neck, the smooth feel of silk brushing against her skin. He watched with a sultry gaze while she swept her hands down over his tie, molding it against her breasts.

She undid his belt buckle and zipper while he slowly unbuttoned his oxford. His tender, controlled gentleness was about to drive her insane. What happened to the aggressive, assertive, take charge Reed she knew? She wanted to scream *Rip off your damn clothes for God's sake!*

He stripped off his shirt, unveiling a soft dusting of black hair spread across his broad muscular chest, and a small crescent-shaped birthmark below one nipple. He removed his pants and she curled her fingers around the top of his boxers and slid them down his legs, onto the floor. Hopefully she appeared in control even though her emotions were running wild, in awe that she was seeing Reed's naked bod.

Using several large red cushions, he made a makeshift bed and guided her onto it. He slid her thong down her legs, his fingers grazing her skin, sending tingles through her entire body. She kicked off her heels, now lying there naked against the soft cushions, except for his tie. He swallowed hard, his gaze caressing her body. His jaw tightened, a muscle twitched, as if his self-control was hanging by a thread. Wearing a sexy, come hither look, she wriggled her body into the comfy cushions and let out a seductive moan. The muscle in his jaw twitched again, but rather than thrusting himself between her legs, he snatched a bottle of Argan oil off the center of the table.

With a seductive, taunting smile, he slowly unscrewed the top of the bottle. She let out a whimper of anticipation. Bottle poised over her stomach, he tilted it slightly, allowing a few drops of oil to land on her stomach. The oil was cool against her warm skin and her stomach muscles tightened. He swirled a finger around in the oil, then brought the finger to her mouth and brushed it over her lower lip. She ran her tongue over his finger, teasing it, savoring the nutty flavor.

He drizzled oil in a circle around her belly and several drops trailed across her skin and puddled in her belly button. He slowly licked the oil from her skin, his tongue playing with her belly button ring. She arched her back, pressing her stomach against his mouth. He continued to leisurely lap up the oil. She curled her fingers into the cushions. Was this some sort of sadistic, albeit incredibly seductive and erotic, Moroccan torture method? She'd *tell* him anything, *do* anything he commanded as long as it involved having him inside her. Now.

In her wildest dreams about Reed, and she'd had plenty, she'd never imagined him so attentive, so focused on satisfying her needs before his own. He seemed intent on pleasuring her when he had to be going out of his mind with desire. This certainly wasn't the straight to the point, get down to business Reed she was used to. Right now, he was making it all about her and she'd never been so attracted to a man in her life.

He trailed kisses up her stomach and over her breasts as he covered her with the warmth of his body. He braced his forearms on either side of her, staring into her eyes. The desire in his blue eyes made her want him a hundred times more. She caressed the back of her hand over his cheek.

"We probably should have had a discussion before we got to this point," he said.

"No condom in your wallet?"

He shook his head. "Sorry."

Good to know he didn't carry condoms in his back pocket, planning on getting lucky. Getting lucky. Oh, yeah. She almost forgot, *she* did carry a condom around. Not because she planned on getting lucky, but she'd gone bar hopping with a bachelorette party on St. Patty's Day. Monica had stuck it in the side pocket of her purse and forgotten all about it.

"I have one."

She reached over and snagged the handle of her purse and dragged it toward her. The clear condom packaging displayed a green condom on the inside, a leprechaun and the words *Do You Feel Lucky* on the outside. Reed eyed the condom with curiosity, a crooked smile quirking the corners of his mouth.

"Got it at a bachelorette party."

He nodded. "Well, it's appropriate. I'm part Irish and certainly feel lucky."

He tore the package open and sheathed his erection in green latex. He slowly lowered his body against hers, the hard plane of his chest molding against her breasts. She got lost in his blue eyes as he slowly slipped inside her. Her breath hitched in her throat. He withdrew then entered again, burying himself deeper. She closed her eyes, letting out a soft moan.

He kissed her, his lips lingering against hers. "Oh yeah, I'm feeling very lucky."

Chapter Nine

The following morning, Monica lay in bed, inhaling the scent of jasmine from Reed's cologne and Argan oil still lingering on her skin. She probably should have showered before going to bed, considering the oil slathered all over her body, and making love to Reed, but she didn't want to wash away his scent. She wanted to sleep immersed in it. Besides, oil was good for her skin.

She slid out of bed, glancing over at the wooden table in the corner displaying the ingredients for her soul mate spell. She hadn't cast the spell in over a week, since Hope had sucked her into creating the dirtbag spell. She couldn't chance Hope popping in again, wanting to cast another negative spell on Kyle.

Did Monica *need* to continue casting it, or had it worked?

Reed couldn't possibly be her soul mate. They were complete opposites. They had nothing in common except being physically compatible. Way compatible. But just because he couldn't be her soul mate and they had no future didn't mean she couldn't enjoy the present, right?

Even though she seriously sucked at flings.

Her gaze focused on the vial of jasmine oil. It wouldn't smell exactly the same as Reed's cologne, but similar. She could dab some on after she showered. She walked over to the table and picked up the small vial of oil. Brushing a finger over the red tablecloth, she recalled her and Reed's bodies intertwined on the red cushions. Red cloth, red cushion. Merely a coincidence or a sign? And the lavender incense reminded her of Reed's shirt the day they'd met, and his purple paisley tie last night.

But the letter she'd written to her soul mate specified she was seeking a fun-loving, spontaneous, open-minded man, who enjoyed the simple things in life like a picnic in the park while watching a dog catch a Frisbee. Not exactly how she'd describe Reed and she couldn't imagine him relaxing enough to lie around in a park all afternoon.

Bummed, Monica went over to the closet and stared down at the empty clothesbaskets. Besides doing laundry on a daily basis, Hope obviously tidied up the closet. The only shoes on the floor were the purple heels from the night before. She'd flung them off her feet while standing in the doorway, and they'd landed like inches from the shoe cubbie. Damn, she was getting good. She stuck them in their designated slot.

She scanned the hanging clothes, instantly matching up a pair of white capris and a magenta wrap shirt. Having her wardrobe organized by colors, and laundered, certainly made getting ready faster in the mornings. Hmm . . . Being more organized might allow her to sleep in another ten minutes. Not being a morning person, that was huge.

She studied the wrinkled shirt. Surprisingly, Hope hadn't ironed it. Steaming out the wrinkles while she showered probably wasn't going to cut it. She suddenly had the urge to iron. She hadn't ironed in like a year and had no clue where her iron was. But Hope's iron and ironing board were in the dining room closet. There went the time she'd gained by being organized.

She zipped downstairs to find Hope dressed in a long, rose-colored sundress with lace trim, her hair tossed up in a pearl clip. She'd probably already done five loads of laundry, baked a cake, and was now devouring the book in her hand titled *Hear Me Roar*. Following her conversation with Reed, she'd gone out and bought a slew of women's empowerment books. Hope focusing her energy on reading, rather than chanting over Kyle's buried sock, was suddenly bringing positive energy into Monica's life.

Hope glanced up from the book. "Hey, how'd last night go? Tried to wait up, but I was dead. Didn't expect you to be so late."

Neither had Monica. Not only had they made love on the *red* cushions, but also on the purple and green ones. And they'd gone through an entire bottle of Argan oil. She ran her tongue across her lips, recalling the nutty flavor of the oil as she'd licked it off Reed's body. Any calories she'd consumed from the oil were well worth it.

"How was the couscous?" Hope asked.

"Great." They'd ravaged it after the second round of lovemaking, needing sustenance for round three. Monica removed the ironing board from the closet, avoiding Hope's gaze as her entire body flushed with memories of the night before.

"So, do you think the event was a huge success?"

"For sure." A whopping four orgasms when she hadn't had *one* in over a year.

Hope's brow creased with concern. "Are you and Reed on okay terms now? If you aren't, I can find another lawyer. I wasn't even thinking about all the problems you two are having when I hired him. Talk about selfish."

Monica couldn't tell Hope about making love to Reed. Not when she'd made a big deal about wanting to get rid of him. And it would be a bit awkward to discuss her four orgasms, and Reed's incredibly sexy bod, when Hope wanted to slice off every protruding part of Kyle's body with a dull metal spatula.

Monica set-up the ironing board. "No, you should let him take Kyle to the cleaners."

"You're sure?"

"Yeah."

Hope set down her book. "I can iron that for you."

"That's okay. I need to learn to iron."

Since when?

*

Monica paced back and forth in her outer office, flicking a hot pink nail against her forehead. She should go see Reed right away, so it didn't seem like she was avoiding him. It would be much more awkward if she didn't run into him for several days. Besides, she really wanted to run into him *now*. She brushed her fingertips over her lips, touching the tip of her tongue to them, recalling licking the Argan oil from Reed's finger, and his reaction. Her body ached for his touch.

Oh yeah, she wanted him *now*.

She peered out the window at the potted lilac bush on the sidewalk between her and Reed's offices. Her good riddance spell had certainly backfired, in a good way. Although, the essence of the spell was to attract positive energy, and the energy between she and Reed while making love had definitely been positive. It had been the most electrically charged, incredible sex ever. How could anything negative come of it?

Being sexually compatible wasn't the issue. The fact that she worked diligently at keeping people together, whereas Reed excelled at permanently separating them, was the issue. Not exactly a minor difference. Not like she had a house full of cats and he had severe dander allergies. Now *that* would be much easier to work through. Neither of them would give up their careers, but maybe if they both made a conscious effort to work through their minor differences—like his anal compulsive tendencies—then their one big difference would somehow work itself out along the way. Doubtful.

Although her parents had learned to give and take. When they'd gotten married her dad had despised Elvis. Now, they made an annual pilgrimage to Graceland, where they currently were. Her mom had quit smoking, since Monica's dad was anti-smoking after losing his dad to lung cancer. They had made concessions for each other in the name of love.

Monica ran a nervous hand over her white cotton capris and magenta wrap shirt, both of them crisply pressed, except for a few iron creases. She needed some practice. But the fact that she suddenly had the urge to iron said a lot.

Was she already subconsciously making concessions for Reed? Worried that her mildly wrinkled appearance bugged him?

She glanced over at Jordan laying out tarot cards on the desk in front of her, conducting Monica's morning reading. "I was thinking, maybe you should install that computer organizer thingy with the calendar and all that other . . . stuff."

Holding a card in mid-air, Jordan glanced up, a stunned expression on her face. When she'd recommended Monica use a software program to get organized, and a computer file rather than sticky notes to store her event ideas, Monica had flat-out refused, afraid being organized would stifle her creative flow of ideas.

"Sure," Jordan finally said. "I'll do that this afternoon, if you promise to stop pacing before I rolf."

Monica stopped pacing. Jordan looked like a Zombie with bloodshot eyes that almost matched the color of her red glasses. She had on zero makeup except for red lipstick, which didn't match her outfit, a major fashion faux pas in itself. A white skirt with brightly colored swirls and a pink shirt with white polka dots. She looked like she'd gotten ready in five minutes flat.

"Too many *Medium Martinis* last night at your psychic social circle?" Monica asked.

Jordan nodded faintly, as if even the slightest movement made her ill.

"What do you guys talk about at those meetings anyway?"

"We exchange recipes for cauldron stews, patterns for voodoo dolls, stuff like that," Jordan said, her voice laced with sarcasm.

She was obviously still ticked over Monica's comment to Reed about torturing his voodoo doll. "I said I was sorry about the voodoo doll thing."

Jordan perked up slightly. "Actually, we came up with a great idea when we were talking about my job here." She fanned her hands out in front of her, looking inspired. "Bring Your Romance

Back to Life. A subdivision of Enhance Your Romance. I could plan events for the dead."

"For the *dead*? Are you for real?" Monica laughed, Jordan didn't. She worked hard to wipe the smile off her face. "Um, how would we get the clients, and who would pay their bills if they're dead? I have a hard enough time getting my *living* clients to pay up."

Jordan looked at Monica like *she* was totally whacked. "The *clients* wouldn't be dead. Their loved ones would be. Like if a woman's husband died right before their fiftieth wedding anniversary, I could plan a special event and contact his spirit to join us for the celebration."

Monica raised a skeptical brow.

"Believe me, people would be all over this. I have a woman who comes to me every year on her husband's birthday. I channel him so she can wish him happy birthday and share a cake with him. I'm telling you, it would be a total hit. At least think about it."

Scary, Jordan might be on to something. She raked in over seventy-five grand a year from people trying to communicate with their deceased loved ones.

"Let's make sure we can service all our living clients first, okay?" They'd had seven messages on the machine that morning thanks to the newspaper article.

"Business is taking off. So why are you so nervous?"

"What if I can't keep up?" Like *that's* what had her pacing. She couldn't tell Jordan she'd made love to Reed. Jordan would insist it was kismet, fate, and that Monica couldn't fight the attraction. That she was destined, or maybe doomed, to be with Reed.

"I can help you plan events. It's not like I'm answering the phone eight hours a day. Although I may be after that article. Even though two of those messages don't count."

One had been from Trish, the scorned woman who'd threatened to sue Monica. She apologized for going berserk and promised she wasn't suing, relieved she'd discovered Jeff was a shithead—along with a dozen other profane names—now rather than later.

Amen.

Monica had felt a sense of relief and . . . disappointment. Losing her business in a lawsuit would have been an out. A better alternative to admitting failure of another business.

The other message had been Jeff, thanking Monica for *introducing* him to Sissy, and wondering if he could get a partial refund since he hadn't actually gone through with the engagement. What a total loser. So was Monica for not making him pay in full in advance. The weasel was likely going to back out on his final payment.

Monica glanced over at the tarot cards on Jordan's desk. Her gaze narrowed on the two of Cups with a man and woman facing each other, holding goblets. She'd had the card upright in a reading a few weeks ago, which represented good partnerships and the kind of sharing that could lead to better things either in business or relationships. She'd assumed it had referred to her and Jordan's working relationship, but could it have been referring to the sharing that took place between she and Reed last night? Rather than upright, the card was now reversed.

"What does that card mean upside down?"

"It usually signifies a couple has the desire to connect, but disagreements and misunderstandings may occur. The problems are solvable, but someone has to make the first move. The need for communication is more important now than ever. It can also signify you're at the point of breaking off a relationship or involved in a passionate situation that you need to keep in check."

No way could Monica keep her passion in check whenever she was around Reed. And she couldn't avoid Reed if the need for communication was critical. She was cosmically torn.

Jordan squinted out the front window. "Isn't that Georgia Marshal?"

Monica glanced out and saw her company's first client stepping from a red Honda Accord. Forty, petite with long blond hair, Georgia had surprised her husband Mike with a romantic dinner for their twentieth anniversary. Both of them Packer fanatics, they'd dined on the fiftieth yard line at the coveted Lambeau Field, wearing autographed jerseys. An event Monica had pulled off thanks to her dad. His company had built the most kick-ass deer stand ever for the Packers coach. The coach had been so thrilled with it he'd told her dad he owed him big time. "Wonder what Georgia's doing here," Monica said. "She paid her bill in full, didn't she?"

"Yep, I can tell you that without looking since she's the only one who has."

She sounded like Hope. But she was right. And after Jeff's fiasco, Monica was definitely getting full payment prior to conducting an event.

Georgia walked toward the office, head down, focused on rummaging through her purse, rather than looking in at Monica. She continued past the office and Monica craned her neck, watching her walk through Reed's door instead.

Were she and Reed friends? Maybe Reed had broken down and called the temp agency for an admin assistant.

"Uh oh," Jordan said, her voice laced with impending doom.

Monica glanced over at her. "What?"

"She's getting a divorce."

"No way." Monica shook her head adamantly. "Georgia and Mike are totally in love. They almost made even me gag the evening of their event, calling each other all these pet names like my *packy wacky baby*."

"So what's she doing there?"

"Probably applying for a temporary admin job."

"She's a hairdresser."

"Maybe she's looking for a change of pace."

"She's looking for a change all right. A change of scenery. She's tired of looking at Mike."

"No way." Monica continued shaking her head as she marched out the door and over to Reed's office.

She peered through the front window, finding the outer office vacant. She slipped quietly through the front door. Luckily there was no buzzer or bell to signal her arrival. The door to his inner office was cracked open and she crept toward it. She flattened herself against the wall outside the office.

"I just want this to be over as quickly as possible," Georgia said. "How long will it take?"

"Three months minimum," Reed said.

"For real? Three months? Can I get it done in Vegas?"

"You have to be a resident there for six weeks before filing for a divorce."

Monica gasped in surprise. Omigod. Jordan was right. Georgia and Mike were getting a divorce. What had happened since their anniversary last month to cause a divorce?

"I don't even want to wait six weeks."

"Believe me, I'll make this as painless as possible. For you anyway."

"How can this be painless?" Georgia let out a sob. "My husband cheated on me."

Cheated?! Monica flung open the door and flew inside, making a beeline for Georgia, avoiding Reed's gaze. "Mike cheated on you?" She plucked a tissue from the box on the desk and handed it to Georgia as she pulled up a chair next to the woman.

Georgia nodded, blowing her nose. "Can you believe it? I just found out."

"You poor thing." Monica placed a consoling hand on her shoulder.

"Um, excuse me," Reed said. "But can I help you?"

"No thanks, I'm not unhappily married," Monica snapped instinctively, without looking at him.

How did this man manage to bring out both the best and the worst in her?

Regretting the snide remark, she slid her gaze over to Reed. Her comment was likely responsible for the hardened look in his blue eyes. The same eyes that had been filled with passion last night.

Georgia blew her nose, reminding Monica of her reason for being in Reed's office. Monica forced her gaze back to Georgia.

"We ran into her at a store. Talk about awkward. I could tell something was up between them. After we left Mike admitted he'd had an affair with her sixteen years ago."

Monica's gaze narrowed. "Sixteen *years* ago?"

"He says it was a one-night stand and it meant nothing."

Monica shot a discreet glance Reed's way. Had last night meant nothing more than a one-night stand for Reed? A sick feeling tossed her stomach. Being one of the most eligible bachelors he likely had his share of flings. If they ran into each other in a store sixteen years from now, would he even remember her name? Worse yet, would he walk right by, not even remembering her *face*?

"Well, it means something to me. Our entire marriage was a lie."

Not that Monica condoned what Mike had done, but they were talking years ago here. Georgia's reaction was a bit drastic, wasn't it? "He never should have done that, Georgia, but are you ready to throw away your marriage of twenty years, which is . . . " She grabbed a gold pen from the holder on the desk and did the math on a tissue. "Which is 7,350 days, over *one* night?"

Georgia rubbed her neck nervously, twisting her mouth around, appearing unsure how to answer. She nodded faintly.

Reed stepped around his desk, toward them. "Can I talk to you outside?" he asked, more of a command than a question.

She ignored his request and focused on Georgia. "When did you find this out?"

"Yesterday."

"This is all too fresh. Take some time to let it settle in. At least a few days. Don't make a drastic decision. What he did is awful, but it was years ago. Obviously things weren't as good then as they are now. What if you regret filing for divorce?"

Georgia wore a torn expression.

"We need to talk." Reed grasped Monica's elbow, propelling

her up from the chair.

"I'll be right back," she said over her shoulder as Reed escorted her into the outer office.

He shut the door behind them. "What are you doing?" His voice was stern, but his grip on her elbow relaxed, his hand remaining, causing her stomach to flutter.

"Please let go of my arm," she finally managed. Before she ripped off his clothes and forgot all about Georgia and her purpose for being there.

Reed slowly lowered his hand from her elbow, staring down at her. *Do not look into his eyes.* She'd be a goner if she looked into his eyes. So instead, she focused on his blue iridescent tie. Thank God it wasn't purple. Her mind flashed back to the night before and draping his purple and pink paisley tie around her neck, the feel of smooth satin against her bare breasts. The feel of his skin and chest hair when she'd fanned her hands across his solid pecs, and brushed a finger over the small crescent shaped birthmark. After three hours of making love she knew every distinguishing freckle, mole, and mark on his body. Every muscle . . .

"How do you know her?" Reed asked, his voice softening.

She raised her gaze to his. Remember, this was business, not personal. "She was my first client."

"Ohhh," he said, nodding, as if that explained everything.

Her gaze narrowed. "Oh, what?"

"It's like when a cop encounters that first case he's unable to solve. He becomes obsessed with it. You have to let it go. Some of your clients are gonna get divorced. Everyone isn't going to grow old together. Shit happens. There's nothing you can do about it. You can't save every relationship out there. Infidelity is the number one grounds for divorce."

Okay, rather than wanting to feel his tie against her naked breasts, she wanted to strangle him with it. "Don't quote me statistics. I just saw them together a month ago. They're totally in love." What had happened to the passionate Reed from the night before, who'd been so in tune with her body, her needs? The cold, calloused, cynical Reed had returned. It was like he had a split personality. Face it. Last night had been about sex for him, not making love. Reed didn't make love, because to him, love didn't exist. An icky taste filled her mouth and she swallowed hard, trying to wash it down. "You can honestly tell me she is in the mind frame to make a decision right now?"

"Going through a divorce is a very emotional and stressful time. I practically spend more on tissues than my office rent."

"Well, maybe you should try listening to what your clients are really telling you rather than what you want to hear."

"Georgia is sitting in *my* office, not *yours*."

"But she should be sitting in mine. I can help her more than you can."

He cocked a brow. "Apparently not."

That was low. She glared at him, unable to believe she'd actually ironed her clothes for this man. "I guarantee I *can* help her. Give me the chance to prove it. Let me plan a romantic event for them and see if there are still feelings to save."

He shook his head like she was completely delusional.

Condescending jerk.

"Afraid I'll prove you wrong?"

He stopped shaking his head, giving her a skeptical, yet slightly defeated look. "It's not up to me. Ask Georgia. If that's what she wants, then go for it."

She smiled confidently. "I will." She took a step toward the office door then stopped. "You know what happened last night can never happen again. We'll never see eye-to-eye on things." She gestured toward his office. If it wasn't Georgia, it would be some other client. Not like they could sit around the dinner table, Reed discussing taking some client's spouse to the cleaners, while Monica talked about taking hers on a romantic sunset cruise.

He nodded, his eyes dimming. "You're right."

Giving in awfully easily wasn't he? Wasn't she worth fighting for? She wanted to search his eyes for even a hint of doubt, but he was gazing down at his tie, picking off an invisible piece of lint. Did avoiding her gaze mean he didn't really think she was right? But she *was* right. They couldn't see each other again. That tarot card was optimistic. They were both too stubborn to give in and neither would make the first move. Jordan had also said the card could be interpreted as a relationship breaking off.

She camouflaged the hurt, hollow feeling inside her with anger, jutting out her chin, squaring her shoulders. "Believe me. I'll help Georgia and Mike. Just wish I could take away all your clients and put you out of business."

"How about three?" he challenged.

Her gaze narrowed. "What do you mean three?"

"If you can convince three couples to change their minds about getting divorced, I'll move."

"Where am I going to find the other two couples?"

"Pretty confident Georgia and Mike are couple number one, aren't you?"

"Yes. I am." She hoped.

"I'll refer two more clients to you I think are on the fence about getting divorced."

"As if I can trust you to do that."

He had the nerve to look offended. "You might not always like what I have to say, but I'm a man of my word. You can trust me."

Amazingly, she trusted him to be honest with her, but not his ability to recognize if a client was on the fence about getting a divorce. He was clueless. Completely out of tune with a woman's emotions. If he weren't, he'd realize she wanted a lot more from him than trust.

Chapter Ten

Monica and Georgia headed toward the front door. Reed's gaze was glued to Monica's white capris, hugging the curves of her ass. He massaged his thumb across his fingertips, his skin rough compared to the smooth, soft feel of hers. The sweet taste of her skin filled his head. He couldn't remember the last time he'd had such mind-blowing sex.

Probably because he never had, not like this.

He'd hardly slept last night, unable to stop thinking about Monica, wishing she was in bed with him, or that they'd spent the night in the restaurant, ducking out early before the first employee arrived. Usually he split after sex, not wanting to give a woman false hopes he'd still be there come morning. Wanting to wake up with Monica in the morning scared him shitless.

He had Monica on the brain, unable to focus on work. A woman had *never* interfered with his job. Natalie Bartolli was due to arrive any minute. He had to get his act together. Get pissed that Monica had just barged into his office and waltzed off with his client, who agreed to hold off filing divorce papers for a few days. Instead, he found her determination and passion for what she believed in sexy as hell. He wasn't worried about her winning their bet. Even on the off chance she did, he was moving his office in two months anyway. So why had he suggested this little game between them? Because it gave him a reason to see her again. And he definitely wanted to see *more* of Monica. Not good.

"Knock, knock," Natalie said, rapping her knuckles on an imaginary closed door.

He really needed to get a bell on the front door.

Natalie sashayed into the office, her blonde hair bouncing

against her shoulders, in rhythm with her step. Medium height, her orange dress hugged every implanted and surgically sculpted curve of her body.

Ignoring his extended hand, she wrapped him in a tight embrace. Her collagen-enhanced lips planted a kiss on his cheek, then brushed one across his lips. Not exactly a step-motherly type kiss. He stood there, unsure how to respond. He wanted to keep their relationship professional, not personal, and certainly not physical. Although screwing over his dad was more personal than professional.

He sat down behind his desk while she sat in the leather chair across from him, elegantly crossing her long legs.

Her green eyes gazed earnestly over at him. "So, you really think I can get more than the two million?"

His father's net worth was conservatively estimated at a cool hundred mil. "Without a doubt. Did you bring your prenup?"

She removed the paperwork from her purse and handed it to him. He skimmed over the six-page document. It dictated that Natalie's weight may never exceed that at the time of their wedding—one hundred and ten pounds. Pretty stringent considering the woman was at least five-four. To maintain her appearance, she had to receive weekly manicures, keep her hair blond and at least shoulder length, and wear contact lenses, never glasses. She would receive cosmetic procedures as needed to maintain a youthful appearance, including chemical peels, liposuction, etc.

Even though their marriage had failed, the prenup had succeeded in making Natalie a beautiful woman, looking more like thirty-five than her actual forty-six. The type of woman Reed would normally go for.

Did that make him as shallow as his father? Hell no! He tightened his grip on the document. He would never mandate that a woman alter her appearance for him. He wouldn't want Monica to plump up her lips with collagen and have the sexy dip over her upper lip disappear. Her hair, just shy of touching her shoulders, was already a perfect chestnut brown. He was addicted to her curves and wouldn't want her to be model thin. He wouldn't want her to change a thing about herself. Especially her strong-willed and independent nature, which would tell him to go to hell if he asked her to shoot herself up with unnatural fillers or color her hair.

But he wasn't dating Monica, was he?

The agreement also required Natalie to be well-rounded. Keeping up on current events, so she could intelligently converse at dinner parties. Participating in cultural events, and volunteering a minimum of one hundred hours a year, making them appear to be a civic minded couple. And most importantly, in bold letters, she would be required to do whatever it took to ensure his business was a success. If she held up her end of the bargain, she'd receive a hundred grand for every year of the marriage. The two million settlement was a nice chunk of change, except when compared to his father's net worth. No mention as to the ramifications of his father having been unfaithful who knows how many times. No mention of his father whatsoever.

He glanced over at Natalie, who was peering into a compact mirror, applying peach-colored lipstick. "This agreement is completely one-sided."

Natalie nodded, snapping the mirror shut. "I know. But I was so excited he was giving me all that money to look good that it seemed like a great deal. And I never dreamed he'd ever make so much money. Of course, I loved him, also, and he wouldn't have married me unless I signed it. He tells me this two nights before we got married."

The process had been rushed and she'd signed under duress. Definitely a point in their favor to help render the prenup void. It had been witnessed by a different lawyer than his father's. "How'd you get a lawyer to review it so quickly?"

"He was Vinnie's friend in town from California for the

wedding. If I'd known at the time what he'd done to you and your mother, I'd have made sure I was better provided for. I honestly believed he regretted what he did to you two. Still do."

How could she think his father had any redeeming qualities after what he'd done to her?

"Not telling you about us and his support payments falls under the open and honest disclosure of all assets and liabilities prior to marriage."

Although he'd paid shit for child support and alimony, he hadn't disclosed this monthly payout to Natalie, who'd obviously had zero involvement in their finances. Not as major as hiding assets from her, but one more point in their favor for getting a judge to overturn the prenup. Prenups were uncommon in Milwaukee, making it easier for Reed to expose loopholes, present precedence from other cases, and convince a judge to take his client's side.

He smiled, the taste of victory filling his mouth.

His father was screwed.

"I helped him build his business and I should be paid for it. I should get a minimum of three grand for every dinner party I held. That's at least what a caterer would charge. And I figure I did an average of ten a year." She handed him a sheet of paper detailing her calculations and how she arrived at the figure due. "I was his travel companion, escorting him on several business trips a year. A personal shopper, buying his suits. I figure I have at least five million coming. I realize I cheated on him, but still, that was the only thing I reneged on and it was only to get him to notice me. Besides, who knows how many times *he* cheated on *me*."

A hurt expression washed over her face. "I can't believe he took that woman to our condo in Aspen. I loved that condo. The shopping in Aspen is to die for. And Vinnie and I used to spend hours in the hot tub. He was a wonderful lover, always so attentive."

Way more than he needed to know.

"One time we made love for two hours in the hot tub, then when we went back inside Vinnie had a romantic dinner all set."

She sniffled, eyeing the tissue box on the desk. "I don't understand why he slept with that other woman. I mean, I never said no to sex."

Surprisingly, that hadn't been a provision of the prenup. Reed had seen that one before. A client requiring his wife to have sex on demand, a minimum of four times a month. Kind of sucked the romance out of a marriage. A prenup should promote open communication and discussion on topics like finances and expectations before marriage. That was the purpose of it. Not to transform a person into your idea of a flawless spouse.

"Maybe he'll realize how good he had it with me. Maybe he'll miss the sex. Maybe he'll come around."

Was she serious?

A distressed moan escaped up her throat as she plucked a tissue from the box. Her eyes watered. "I don't want him to get the condo and have to think about him and that woman in the hot tub. Do you think there's any way I could get the condo in the settlement so I can sell it?"

"Likely."

This perked her up a bit. "When he used to tell his accountant to claim the place as a business expense I always wondered what business he did there. I didn't realize he meant funny business. It sure wasn't for any other kind of business."

Now that was interesting. How many other bogus write-offs had his father taken over the years? Even if a judge didn't agree with the holes in the prenup, Reed could threaten his father with tax fraud. Some might consider that extortion. Reed thought of it as leverage, to ensure an expedient and lucrative settlement.

Although, his father going to prison might be worth a helluva lot more than half his net worth.

Chapter Eleven

Late that afternoon, Monica sat at her desk, finalizing her plans for Georgia and Mike's romantic event the following evening. Time was of the essence. She had to conduct the event before Georgia impulsively decided to go through with the divorce, even though she'd promised to think things over for a few days.

After leaving Reed's office, Monica had phoned Mike to offer her creative talent. He'd teared up on the phone and promised to do whatever it took to win Georgia back, including marrying her all over again. This gave Monica the idea to have him propose again and renew their wedding vows—since he hadn't stuck by them the first time. Kind of like a *vow cleansing*.

Their first date had been at the art museum, a Monet special exhibition. Mike wasn't big on art, but Georgia was. Another example of a guy making concessions in the name of love. So Monica called her friend, an art professor at the university, for the name of a talented, destitute student who would work for cheap. He'd recommended a guy named Tad, who would be drawing portraits at Bastille Days, the French festival kicking off the following day. She'd phoned Tad and offered him a hundred bucks to draw Georgia and Mike's portrait when they "happened" upon him at the festival, including a blurb asking Georgia to marry Mike. Tad had eagerly accepted the job. She'd then phoned Mike and advised him of the plan.

She planned to arrive at the festival early and hunt down a strolling violinist or accordion player to add the finishing touch. This event had to be perfect. She was determined to prove Reed wrong. To say I told you so. Of course, most importantly, to keep Georgia and Mike together.

But what if the event was a total bust? She couldn't seem to execute a flawless event lately. What if Georgia was hot for Tad and chose Tad over Mike like Jeff had chosen Sissy over Trish? She should have asked Craig for a homely artist. She opened up her top desk drawer and pulled out the charm bag. She swept it under her nose, ODing on the scent of jasmine as her mind flooded with memories of Reed removing her panties . . .

Stop! Stop thinking about making love with Reed. They'd both agreed it could never happen again. She needed to create a new charm bag without the scent of jasmine. Yet, she raised the bag to her nose, preparing to take another deep breath when Jordan breezed through the door.

"I've got it." Jordan shook a CD in her hand. "The software for the computer organizer. I just installed it on my computer."

"Oh, I think I changed my mind."

"I paid forty-nine bucks for this. I'm installing it and you're gonna like it. Now move it." She gestured for Monica to vacate her chair. "If I have to burn every sticky note in a ten-mile radius, you are using this program. Oh, burn, that reminds me." She went back out to her desk and returned, handing Monica a box of patchouli incense sticks and a patchouli oil roll-on perfume. "They didn't have any spray."

Monica eyed the perfume. "What am I supposed to do, roll this over the leaves?"

"Will make it last a lot longer than being able to dump it over the entire bush. Now let me install this."

Monica reluctantly pushed herself up from the chair. This organizer certainly wasn't a concession she was making on Reed's behalf. Besides planning Georgia and Mike's event, she had nine new clients. Being more organized was critical to growing her company. Plain and simple.

She snagged the book of matches she had in her desk drawer for lighting candles, and armed with the patchouli incense, walked outside to the lilac bush. She stuck a stick in the soil, angling it away from the blooms of the bush, not wanting it to catch fire. By the time she was done arranging the incense in the soil, it looked like she was playing a game of pick-up sticks. She lit the ends one at a time and blew them out. Lazy, wisps of smoke drifted up, wrapping around each other, curling together in a cloud hovering over the bush. She closed her eyes and inhaled a deep breath. The exotic, musky scent filtered through her body, easing her muscles into total submission.

"Getting a little desperate?" Reed asked, his voice low and raspy, and oh so close to her.

Her eyes shot open and she spied him out of the corner of her eye, a foot away at most. The scent of his cologne somehow managed to infiltrate the thick cloud of patchouli, which suddenly seemed to drift up her body, caressing it, taking on a sensual scent, evoking thoughts of Reed's naked body wrapped around hers, inside hers . . .

She gave herself a mental shake. This bush was supposed to be keeping them apart, not bringing them closer together. She swallowed hard then peered over at Reed, who was eying her with interest. His gaze grew more intense as she leaned toward him, quirking a suggestive brow, flashing him a cocky, albeit flirty grin.

"Ah, no," she said. "If I were *desperate,* I'd want you to *stick* around." The sexual innuendo wasn't lost on him and he looked surprised by her comeback, no smart-ass reply.

She spun around and marched inside, her legs so shaky she was sure they would collapse.

Her purpose for getting rid of Reed was no longer merely professional, it was personal. She was becoming more concerned about him destroying her heart than her business.

*

When Monica arrived home, a spicy aroma and sizzling sound led her to the kitchen. Hope was stirring vegetables and chicken around in a wok on the counter, while reading a book titled *It Isn't You, It's Him.*

Hope glanced up from the book. "Reed is right. Kyle will fail while I succeed." However, a flicker of doubt in her eyes betrayed her self-confident tone. She set down the book. "Do you like chicken stir-fry?"

"Love it."

"Thought we could eat outside."

Monica peered out the sliding doors at the white plastic table and chairs on the patio. Hope must have gone back to her house for more stuff.

Hope popped a piece of chicken in her mouth then added more sauce to the wok. "I'm going to have to get a full-time job to survive. I'm not going to make it working part time. The problem with my job is it's not like being a hairdresser where you have established clients you see on a monthly basis. My business is a one-time thing. Well, usually. I just made Rachel Donovan a cake for her third wedding. If I don't start getting more clients, I'm gonna have to look for a different career."

If Hope worked full time, who was going to keep Monica's hamper empty and cook dinner?

Omigod, Monica was getting as spoiled as Kyle.

"I could refer some business your way. Whenever I plan an engagement proposal, I could give them your business card."

Since hiring Reed two days ago, Hope seemed to be doing better emotionally, so she probably wouldn't be mutilating any innocent wedding cakes.

"That'd be super."

"Have you thought about opening a bakery slash cake decorating shop?"

"I couldn't run a major business like that." Hope stopped stirring the contents of the wok and glanced over at Monica. "Could I?"

"If Kyle can operate a restaurant, you can run a business."

"Kyle took over the restaurant from his parents. It's not like he started it from scratch."

"You established a successful part-time business. I've started enough businesses, I could do it in my sleep. I'll give you some pointers."

Hope smiled. "Hmm . . . maybe. I'm just not sure if I want to decorate cakes full time. When I went to that wedding Saturday and watched the bride march down the aisle I wasn't thinking 'Ohhh, how beautiful,' I was thinking, 'How long until he cheats on her?'"

Wow. Hope had hit rock bottom.

"Maybe it's time for a career change. Wish I'd never let Kyle talk me out of going back to college, telling me it didn't take a degree to bake cakes. As if that was all I was capable of doing."

"Running a part-time business has given you a ton of transferable skills. And you did the restaurant's accounting. I can pay you for handling my accounting. Not a lot, but I got eight more clients today so I'll be bringing in more money."

The phone rang out on the pedestal table. Monica went to answer it and Hope held out a halting hand. "Don't. It's Kyle. He's been calling all day."

Following three more rings, Kyle's voice blared out of the answering machine. "I know you're there, Hope. Answer the friggin' phone. We need to talk. Now. I—"

Monica turned down the volume on the machine, shutting Kyle up. She needed to look into changing her number. "What's he so ticked off about?"

"Probably been getting more phone calls on the items I put in the paper last weekend. I'm no expert, but I'd guess eight grand for his new Harley is a steal."

Undoubtedly.

"I can't wait for the divorce settlement. I need money *now* until I can get a full-time job."

Hope and Kyle had little in savings because most of it was tied up in the house, restaurant, and Kyle's toys. Luckily, they hadn't signed a prenup so fifty percent of everything was Hope's. Kyle would undoubtedly try to screw her out of her fair share. Good thing she had Reed on her side.

A half hour later, they were lounging out on the patio, brainstorming Hope's new business, enjoying piña coladas, when a motorcycle roared up the street and stopped out front.

Hope craned her neck, peering around the corner of the house. Her body tensed, her fingers tightening around the drink glass. "It's Kyle." Her gaze darted around like she was considering making a run for it. She'd only talked to him that one time on the phone and didn't look ready to confront him face-to-face.

"You can do this," Monica said. "Remember, Kyle will continue to fail while you succeed. You can accomplish whatever you set your mind to. There's nothing you can't do . . . " she rattled off Reed's little pep talk and an air of confidence spread over Hope's face.

Hope nodded. "I can do this. I will succeed. "

Moments later Kyle appeared, bearing a strong resemblance to the *Wild Man of Borneo,* straight out of the jungle; unshaven, unshowered, and frighteningly unstable.

"See your bike hasn't sold," Monica said. "Guess maybe we should list it in the paper at five grand this week."

"Where the hell is it?" Kyle growled, practically foaming at the mouth, raking a hand through his mess of blond hair.

Monica's top lip curled back in disgust. "Buy yourself another stinking Rolex, would you? We're not giving yours back. It'll break the spell."

He looked at her like she was nuts. "I'm talking about my Range Rover. You better not have sold it."

"How could we sell it?" Hope piped up. "Your name's on the title."

He paused a beat. "You probably forged it."

"Get a grip," Monica said.

His head snapped over to Monica. "Screw you. This is all your fault."

"My fault? I'm not the one who was cheating. Or are you referring to the spell I helped Hope with?"

"Your spell's a crock of shit." Kyle's face twitched and he scratched it. From the red blotches covering his cheeks, it appeared he'd been itching a lot. "I was referring to you putting my obit in the paper and robbing my house."

Whatever. Monica hadn't helped Hope with the obit, the classified ads, or moving.

"*Your* house!" Hope was out of her chair. "That house is fifty percent mine. So is the Range Rover, but I didn't touch the stupid thing."

"Must have gotten stolen," Monica said. "Still don't believe in spells?"

"I'm not leaving until you tell me what you did with it." Kyle dropped down in a chair and crossed his arms over his chest. He scratched his face.

"Quite an itch you've got there," Monica said. "What other symptoms are you having?"

"Symptoms? What the hell you talking about?"

"The flesh eating disease you died from in your obit." She had no clue what the symptoms were, but it seemed reasonable that itching would be one of them.

"That obit was bogus. I don't have no stupid flesh eating disease."

"Oh wow." Hope's eyes widened with realization. "The spell was only supposed to warn women about him."

"And keep them from finding him attractive," Monica mused. "What woman is going to want him with half his flesh missing?" She shook her head, staring nervously at Kyle's face. "Doesn't look good." Had the negative energy from the spell returned tenfold, but to Kyle rather than Monica?

Kyle scratched his face. "I don't believe in black magic."

Monica glanced down at his jeans zipper. "Is your face the only thing itching?"

Kyle's gaze darted to his zipper, a freaked out look on his face. He surged from his chair. "What the hell is in the water around here? You're all a bunch of nutcases. I'm going to the police and filing a report on my Range Rover." He turned to Hope. "So you can be expecting a visit from them real soon."

"Might want to stop off at the doctor first and get something for that itch," Monica said.

Kyle's face twitched. "You won't get away with this." He stormed off.

Monica turned to Hope. "What'd you do with the Range Rover?"

Hope shook her head. "Didn't touch it. Kyle wanted that stupid thing not me." She held out a trembling hand. "Can't believe I just talked to him like that. I didn't sound nervous, did I?"

Monica shook her head. "Not at all." She'd never seen Hope stand up to Kyle no matter how big of an ass he was.

Hope dropped back in the chair, looking pleased with herself and Kyle's physical state. "He looked awful, didn't he?"

Monica nodded. "Like total crap."

Monica had once believed Kyle and Hope were the perfect match. Until their cousin Megan had caught him having sex with some chick in the women's bathroom at a Springsteen concert a few years ago. He'd been boffing her in the bathroom stall.They'd walked out of the stall, Kyle zipping his jeans, the girl hooking her bra, and upon seeing Megan, he'd claimed she was his friend's girlfriend and he was holding her hair back while she'd puked her guts out. Hope had totally bought his story, along with several other lame ones over the past few years. She'd refused to believe he was a no-good cheating bastard until last week when she'd caught him in the act.

What if Mike was lying and he'd cheated on Georgia more than once over the past sixteen years? What if Monica was getting them back together when he was actually a total slime like Kyle? What if Reed was right?

Omigod. She was becoming as cynical as Hope and Reed.

Chapter Twelve

Monica zipped past a fifty-foot tall replica of the Eiffel Tower rising majestically in the middle of the downtown square, the focal point of the Bastille Day festivities. She'd touched base with Tad and given him a description of Mike and Georgia. He drew both caricatures and portraits. She'd requested a portrait, since a cartoon drawing—an unflattering distortion of reality to boot—was hardly romantic.

Monica poured the remainder of her bottled water into her palm, then flicked it on her face with her fingers. The humidity was stifling. Like trying to breathe with a wet washcloth stuffed in her mouth. After a month without rain, the grass on the main square felt like glass splinters poking through her sandals. Much of the festival was held on the blacktopped streets surrounding the square, cranking the temperature up another ten degrees. She glanced up at the dark clouds hovering above, praying the rain held off since she didn't have a back-up location in case of inclement weather.

Sweat was seeping out of every pore, a combination of the heat and nervousness. She took a few calming breaths. This event had to be flawless. She'd told Mike that Tad would be stationed first in the line of artists starting on the south side of Jackson Street. So unless he went to the wrong artist, what else could go wrong? She glanced up at the dark clouds then in the direction of the artists. Tad could agree to draw another couple right before Georgia and Mike got there, and Georgia wouldn't want to wait for him. Or maybe Georgia had refused to even come with Mike period. What if Georgia showed, but turned down Mike's proposal of renewing their vows?

A *ton* of things could go wrong.

The can-can song drifted over from a stage in the distance. Her client had loved the idea of performing the can-can and flashing her boyfriend in the audience with *Will You Marry Me Tom?* at the end of the dance. However, the words wouldn't all fit on a pair of frilly undies, so Monica had them embroidered on the back underside of the skirt, visible when she lifted it high in the air at the end.

Monica passed a crowd congregating around a mime performing on a street corner. Dressed in a black and white striped shirt, black beret, and black pants, his face was painted white, his lips red. A female violinist strolled by playing "La Vie en Rose" and the mime assumed the role of a star-struck lover, batting his eyelashes and flirting with the violinist.

"Ever been to Paris?" Reed asked, startling her.

She'd successfully avoided him all day until encountering him when she left the office. She'd made the mistake of telling him she was off to Bastille Days to reunite Georgia and Mike.

"What are you doing here?" she snapped.

He'd exchanged his black suit for jeans and a black T-shirt. Even out of his power suit, and despite the ninety percent humidity, he still had that cool, confident air about him. Confidence that Monica would fail at reconciling Georgia and Mike, no doubt. If this event was a total bust, Reed was there to witness its failure, gloat in victory, and say I told you so.

"Georgia is technically my client also," he said. "I was curious to see how this all turns out."

She smiled sweetly. "Well, go on back to your office," she made a shooing motion with her hand, "and when Georgia doesn't show up there you'll know it all turned out fine." She focused her attention back on the mime. As best as she could anyway with Reed standing so close.

The mime pulled a bouquet of plastic flowers from a violin case on the ground. He scanned the crowd as he marched around the perimeter, imitating a bride marching down the aisle. He stopped in front of her and Reed, presenting Reed the bouquet. Reed thanked him and the mime gave his eyes an exaggerated roll, nudging Reed toward Monica. The onlookers laughed. Reed handed her the bouquet, gazing deep into her eyes. The last guy who'd given her flowers had been Luke Sawyer in high school. His family had managed a cemetery and he'd swiped them off a grave, failing to remove the "Rest in Peace" ribbon tied around the stems.

The mime placed a hand to his chest, an *Ahhh* expression on his face. Upon his direction, the crowd went "Ahhh," in unison.

All eyes were on them and Monica could feel her body temp rising another ten degrees, her cheeks turning pink. The mime plucked a *real* long stemmed red rose hidden within the bouquet of plastic flowers and handed it to Reed, who in turn presented it to Monica. The mime leaned in and carefully separated the petals, peering at the center of the rose. Eyes widening, he placed a hand over his mouth in awe. Monica and Reed glanced inside the flower to find a tiny note written in French.

Je t'aime.

"I love you," Reed said.

Heart racing, Monica's gaze darted up to his.

"That's what it says," he clarified, his gaze never wavering from hers.

Monica smiled faintly. "I figured that."

Then why was her heart hammering in her chest and his words *I love you* echoing through her head? Even though he'd merely been translating, and they were the mime's words, not his, they'd sounded sincere, full of meaning, of passion. It had to be her imagination that he'd said the words with such feeling. He would never say he loved her and mean it. Great sex didn't constitute love, or even like. It was about lust.

Still, she liked the way he'd said *I love you . . .*

She swallowed hard. "This would make an incredible engagement proposal." Changing the subject to business was a sure way to extinguish any heat between them.

"Yeah, it would."

She held the rose out to the mime and he shook his head adamantly, pushing the flower back toward her. He pointed at the bouquet of plastic flowers. She handed them over, glad to keep the rose.

"Do you have a business card?" she asked him.

His bright red lips spread into a gleeful smile. He did a happy little jaunt over to the violin case and produced a card from it. He returned and presented it to her. She thanked him and he continued entertaining the crowd.

She glanced down at her watch, gnawing at her lower lip. Only fifteen minutes until show time. The mime's performance had given her mind a needed break from scrolling through the potential disasters she may soon encounter.

"What's wrong?" Reed asked.

"Nothing," she said with false confidence.

She could *not* let Reed see her sweat. She could do this. She was in control. Did Reed ever feel out of control? Did his emotions ever get the best of him? Was he merely putting on a cool façade to cover up feelings of anxiety and uncertainty? If something did go wrong, she could not freak out and lose it in front of him. Like she had twice before.

Shoulders squared, she attempted to exude confidence, hoping not only to convince Reed everything would be fine, but also herself. "I have to head over to the artists. Georgia and Mike should be arriving soon." She started walking off.

"Sounds good." He followed after her.

She stopped, turning to him. "You can't come with me. She'll know something's up. I'm pretending like I'm happening upon them by accident."

"Like I happened upon you? We can happen upon them together. This is a popular event. Half the city's here."

"She saw the way we acted toward each other in your office yesterday, she knows we don't get along," she said, trying another angle. "Not like we'd be walking around some romantic festival together."

"We sounded like a typical couple arguing."

"We are so not a typical couple."

He arched a curious brow, as if to say, *Exactly what sort of couple are we?*

"We aren't any sort of couple." She let out a frustrated groan. No time to argue, she took off toward the artists on the opposite side of the square.

Reed made idle chitchat, while she pretended not to listen. He commented on the delicious looking pastries displayed in food stands, a street performer juggling plastic bottles of wine, and a woman dressed like Marie Antoinette, who had to be sweating her corset off and on the verge of passing out from the heat. Safe, mundane topics. They finally encountered the artists, a row of easels lined up one after another next to the curb. They strolled toward Tad on the far end where Mike and Georgia were already posing.

"Hey, you guys," Georgia called out to them.

Monica peered over at Georgia and Mike sitting in the chairs, trying to appear surprised to see them. She gave them a little wave. "Oh, hi."

The couple sat next to each other, but their bodies weren't touching and Georgia looked reserved, distant. The fact that they were even sitting together was a positive sign. Monica let out a discreet sigh of relief.

She peered nonchalantly over Tad's shoulder, studying the drawing. Holy crap! Georgia's nose looked like Doonesbury's. She glanced discreetly over at Georgia. Granted, her nose was kind of long and pointy, but she'd freak when she saw the drawing.

"It looks great," Monica called out to them.

Reed nodded in agreement.

She leaned over to Tad. "This was supposed to be a portrait, not a caricature."

Tad gave her a lazy shrug, an action in tune with his dark

shoulder length hair, five o'clock shadow, and wrinkled *Kiss Me I'm French* white tee. "The dude wanted a caricature."

What was Mike thinking? Georgia would never agree to renew her vows with a man who allowed her flaws to be magnified tenfold!

Monica took a deep breath. Remain calm. In control.

"Maybe I'll have a drawing done. But *smaller*," she said, emphasizing the word as she discreetly gestured toward Georgia's nose. "Much smaller."

Tad's easy going smile tightened, but he took an eraser off his stand and proceeded to downsize her nose. She was paying double his going rate, she had the right to micro manage.

She glanced over at the couple. "We're gonna check out the other artists. See ya around." Monica and Reed moved on, pretending to watch other artists at work.

"See, it's going fine," Reed said.

"Didn't say it wasn't."

"You seem nervous."

"Ah, no, I'm not nervous." Her voice cracked.

"How can you have more faith in love and marriage than in yourself?"

She gave him an incredulous look, like he was totally clueless. "I have faith in myself." She knew the meltdowns she'd had in his office after the Renaissance Faire and at the Casbah would come back to haunt her.

"You should. You're very creative. I could never begin to do what you do."

"Well, planning creative ways to serve divorce papers probably isn't a job requirement."

He smiled. "Creativity is a natural talent, it can't be learned. Whereas executing a successful event, troubleshooting, like what you just did, comes with experience."

"It's also made me a pessimist. Always planning for the worst-case scenario."

"That's not pessimistic, it's being proactive, and smart. Shit happens. It's being able to do damage control when it does that matters. You're very good at what you do." He sounded like he was arguing a case in front of a judge, supplying the cold hard facts, leaving no room for dispute. "Your business is gonna do well."

Whoa. Wait a sec. Reed Walker was impressed with her abilities? He respected her? Even after she'd admitted in the restaurant the other night that she'd had thirteen business plans fail he still thought she could be a success?

He had more faith in her than she had in herself.

A sense of confidence slowly crept over her, bringing a smile to her lips.

She could do this.

She peered over at Reed, even more attracted to him than when they'd made love. And this time she couldn't blame it on the jasmine scent of his cologne, his blue eyes, his incredible bod, or anything *physical.*

This was so not good.

"We should go see how Tad's doing," she said, coming to an abrupt halt and heading back in the opposite direction.

She speed walked back to Tad. The drawing of Mike resembled the cartoon character Johnny Bravo, with a big square head. Since a caricature had been his bright idea, he was on his own. If Monica were going to tick off Tad, it would be for Georgia's sake. The woman's nose was better—not great, but better. However, her hair looked like a bush woman's. Kind of how Kyle's had looked last night. Monica glanced over at Georgia. Humidity was wreaking havoc on her hair, which was long and blond, and on a good day looked a bit like Kate Hudson's.

"You're hair looks like Kate Hudson's," Monica told her.

"Thanks." Georgia smiled, smoothing a hand over her hair.

"Doesn't her hair look like Kate Hudson's?" she asked Tad, pointing at the drawing. "Long and *silky smooth.*"

Tad's jaw tightened, but he started erasing.

"Wonder where the accordion player is," she said softly.

"Isn't that him?" Reed nodded to an older gentleman dressed in black with a black beret and an accordion, looking their way.

"Oh, yeah."

The guy gave her a wink, confirming he was set.

Tad put on the finishing touches, including a collage of Parisian landmarks in the background, the Eiffel Tower and the Arch of Triumph. The blurb coming out of Mike's mouth read *Will You Marry Me Again Georgia?*

Not Virginia, or Louisiana, but *Georgia*. The right state and name. Monica breathed a sigh of relief.

"*C'est finit,*" Tad said proudly. He glanced over at Monica for confirmation that he was indeed done.

"*Oui,*" she said, nodding. It looked perfect.

The couple slid off their chairs and walked over to them. Georgia studied the drawing. "Wow, I look way better than I expected. And you . . . " She read the caption and tears instantly materialized in her eyes. She slowly turned to Mike, a cautious look in her blue eyes.

"I'm so sorry, baby," Mike said, tearing up himself. "But I can't live without you."

The accordion player approached, right on cue, and began playing "La Vie En Rose." Monica glanced down at the rose in her hand. She should have had roses for Mike to give Georgia. She raised the rose, preparing to hand it to Mike, but then lowered it. She didn't want to give it away. She wanted to press it inside a book, preserving it forever, along with the memory of Reed saying I love you.

Georgia nibbled at her lower lip, a tear slipping down her cheek. Come on Georgia, forgive him.

"I need some time." Georgia swallowed back a sob. "But I don't think I can live without you, either." Mike wrapped his arms around her, enveloping her in an embrace.

People gathered around to check out what was going on. A guy told Mike his proposal rocked and Mike gave Monica credit. Monica received requests for several business cards.

"Guess you only need to save two more marriages and I'm gone," Reed said, a hint of disappointment in his voice.

Disappointment over having to move or losing a client?

He watched Georgia and Mike, a pleased expression on his face. He appeared happy with the outcome of their relationship. Every time she thought she had him pegged as a heartless bastard he proved her wrong. Was there a true romantic beneath his scorned and cynical exterior? If so, how did she get to it?

"Guess so," she agreed weakly.

She should feel more victorious than she did. Of course it felt great to have had a hand in Georgia and Mike reconciling, but not in evicting Reed from his office. Even though it was the best thing for her business. She couldn't afford to have any more golf-wielding Marjories taking out clients' car windows or lipstick vandals defacing her office window. Yet, deep down, she hoped she couldn't trust Reed to refer two more potential clients her way.

*

Reed watched the couple hugging, tears streaming down both of their faces. He was used to clients, both men and women, getting emotional, but usually it was tears of anger or hurt. Tears of joy were a nice change. Yesterday, Georgia had sat in his office planning to file for divorce, and today she couldn't live without this guy. Thanks to Monica's intervention.

Could some of his other clients possibly have worked things out? Maybe he was too quick to push people into a divorce. But they shouldn't be coming into his office unless they wanted one. He asked clients flat out in the initial consultation if there was any chance of a reconciliation. On a few occasions, clients had confessed they hoped to work things out with their spouses. He advised them to seek marriage counseling. He didn't want to waste his time on clients who weren't serious about getting divorced.

If Georgia and Mike got counseling, maybe they'd discover Monica had merely prolonged the inevitable and they'd go through with the divorce. Georgia said she needed some time to think. Maybe she'd be back in his office in another week.

He hoped like hell that wasn't the case.

Monica wore a dreamy expression. High on romance. "I'm going to get some champagne."

"Think I'll join you."

She looked surprised and a bit confused. "This really isn't something for you to be celebrating, is it?"

"It turned out to be the right thing for Georgia, so it's a good thing."

She nodded slowly, as if trying to process his comment. "Ah, okay."

En route to the champagne booth, they passed by the mime. When Reed had translated the I love you note for Monica, nervous anticipation had his heart pounding like a son of a bitch, and he'd about broken out in a cold sweat, as if he was waiting for her to repeat the words to him. That was insane. Two women had uttered those words to him and he'd dropped them faster than five grand in an Armani store. He'd never spoken those words to a woman. However, saying them to Monica had felt right. What the hell? He hadn't even known her a week. Not like he loved her. She drove him crazy. Half the time he didn't know if he wanted to kiss her or beat his head against a wall. He was in lust with her. That was it.

"Isn't that your mom?" Monica said, directing the rose in her hand toward a crepe stand.

It was indeed his mother and Bill standing in line, holding hands, laughing. Bill had on a blue floral Hawaiian shirt. The type of shirt that should only be worn to a luau in Hawaii. Reed added shitty dresser to his list of issues with the guy.

"Yeah, it is."

They walked over to them.

"*Bonjour*," Monica said.

"Well, *bonjour*," his mother said.

His mother and Monica hugged. Reed gave Bill an awkward nod hello then introduced him to Monica. In his mid-fifties, Bill was in decent shape, tall, with short gray hair.

A hopeful smile on her face, his mother glanced between him and Monica. He knew that meddling look. She was reading more than she should into them being there together. His purpose there was strictly work related. At least that's what he told himself.

"Where'd you get the rose from?" she asked Monica, glancing expectantly over at Reed.

Monica explained the mime skit.

"How romantic," his mother said.

"It was just a skit," Reed assured her, not wanting her to get her hopes up or she'd have them as good as married. She looked disappointed by this, as did Monica. Had Monica wanted it to be more than a skit?

"I'm glad to see you two here together. I was afraid the awkward situation the other day with Ms. Reynolds might have you on the outs." She turned to Monica. "I'm so sorry about that."

"Don't worry about it. You didn't know. It worked out . . . fine." Monica's cheeks and neck flushed a bright pink and she avoided Reed's gaze.

Was she thinking back to them making love?

He agreed. The evening had worked out pretty damn well.

He shot a discreet glance to the neckline of Monica's sleeveless purple shirt. The top button undone, a white camisole peeked out from underneath, as did the top of her full breasts.

"Reed's been to Paris several times," his mother said.

Bill slipped an arm around her shoulder, giving it an affectionate squeeze. "We should go there someday."

She leaned her head against his shoulder. "Yes, we should."

The ambiance of the festival seemed to have them acting even more lovey dovey than the other three times Reed had seen them together. He couldn't stomach this right now.

"Speaking of going places," Reed said, "we should get going."

"Why don't you join us for dinner?" his mother said.

"That's okay. We already ate," he lied.

They said goodbye and he and Monica headed toward the champagne booth. They passed a garbage can and Monica whipped the rose in it. She didn't just toss it in, she *whipped* it in, as if throwing away photos of a boyfriend she'd just caught in bed with some other chick. What was that about? Was she pissed he'd said the skit meant nothing? She was the one who'd said they couldn't see each other again and she acted like she didn't even want him here. This woman definitely sent out mixed signals.

"Why did you say we'd already eaten? You don't like Bill?"

He shrugged, noncommittal.

"He seems like a nice guy and looks like he makes your mom happy."

"They've only known each other three months and they're already engaged."

"That's wonderful," she said wistfully.

"He's been divorced four times."

"Oh." She sounded like that took some of the air out of her love balloon. "Guess that's not a great sign. But if your mom's okay with it, then that's really all that matters."

"She has no clue he's been married four times."

Monica's gaze narrowed in confusion. "Then how do *you* know that?"

"Never trusted him, so I had him investigated." He peered over at her, expecting to see an appalled expression on her face that he'd gone behind his mother's back. Instead, she looked like she was weighing the negatives against the positives.

"Don't you think you should tell her? She has the right to know. Especially if Bill isn't being honest with her. If I were her, I'd have a bigger issue with him not being up front about his divorces than the divorces themselves."

"She'd be royally pissed at me for having Bill investigated."

"You did it because you care about her. She might be upset at first, but she'd get over it."

He let out a frustrated sigh. "If she'd just agree to a damn prenup, I wouldn't ever have to confront her about it."

"Not knowing Bill's past, I don't blame her for not wanting a prenup. Prenups set up the marriage to fail right from the get go. They're bad luck."

"Not having a prenup is why she got screwed in her first divorce."

Monica paused a moment, appearing to think over her next comment. "Your father?"

He nodded. "Don't wanna talk about it." His jaw tightened and a vile taste filled his mouth, like every time he thought about the bastard. "He's not around anymore." Not around Reed anyway, except in court. He sure as hell didn't want Monica to know who his father was. Hopefully she never would since the discovery of his tax evasion gave Reed leverage to ensure a quick and quiet settlement. "A prenup protects both parties. It grounds the marriage in realistic expectations. Forces partners to have open and honest discussions and respect what each partner wants from the marriage. Lack of communication is one of the biggest causes of a marriage failing."

"Yeah, but still . . . " The defensive look on her face faded away as her voice trailed off.

"Wouldn't you want to protect your business? What if you got divorced and a vindictive husband got half the business when it was your hard work and money that built the company from scratch? Or what if your husband ran up a debt and you had to sell your company to help pay it off?"

Gaze narrowed, she twisted her mouth around, looking like she was trying hard not to see the upside to a prenup. "I should probably skip the champagne and get going. Have a lot of work to do tonight."

Usually that was his line. And he did have a lot of work to do, but he wasn't about to use the line on Monica even though it was true.

She held up a palm, peering at the overcast sky. "Besides, I feel sprinkles."

Along with the dark clouds, dusk was settling in. He didn't want her walking around alone. "I'll walk you to your scooter. Where you parked?"

She gestured north of the square. "Over there somewhere. But I'll be fine."

"I don't mind. I'm parked in the same area." Now he knew why he'd driven around for ten minutes until he'd spotted her scooter.

She relented and they headed in the direction of the parking lot. An accordion's rendition of "Under the Paris Sky" followed them down a tree-lined path between two buildings. A raindrop landed on the top of Reed's upper lip and he wiped it away. A few more drops hit his cheeks. Monica swept her fingertips across her cheek, obviously feeling the drops also. They exchanged glances, simultaneously picking up their pace.

Sprinkles turned into a steady stream of rain within seconds flat. He grasped hold of Monica's hand and they made a dash for a green awning covering the back entrance to a building. He maintained a brisk jog, rather than the sprint he'd have done if Monica weren't by his side. He ran five miles every morning, except if it rained. Then he hit the treadmill. As they neared the awning the sky opened up, unleashing sheets of rain down on them. They reached cover, their bodies slick with rain. Still holding Monica's hand, he raked his other hand through his wet, mussed up hair and Monica pushed a clump of matted hair from her forehead. Rather than bitching about her hairdo being completely jagged, she began giggling.

"Omigod," she said between giggles, "does that feel awesome. I am so freakin' hot."

She slipped her hand from his and he wanted to protest until she began removing her purple cotton shirt, revealing the white spandex camisole underneath. He envied the camisole hugging her body, molding to her every curve. He was about to wrap his arms around her waist and pull her to him when she tossed her purple shirt on the ground and darted back out into the rain. Tilting her head toward the sky, rain sluiced over her. Eyes closed, she opened her mouth, slipping out her tongue, catching a steady stream of raindrops on it. She swept her hands up over her forehead, smoothing her wet hair back from her face, looking like some mythical mermaid who'd just surfaced from beneath the ocean.

Her eyes fluttered open, blinking away the raindrops. She glanced over at him, raindrops trailing over her lips, a sultry look on her face. "Come on. It feels great."

He hadn't played out in the rain since he was like nine. Without hesitation, he stepped from the shelter of the awning and joined her. Her eyes filled with surprise and a slow, sexy as hell smile curled the corners of her mouth. She stared up at him, blinking raindrops off her long lashes, sweeping her tongue across the perfect dip over her lip.

"Feels good, doesn't it?" she asked in a breathless tone.

Oh yeah, he nodded. He'd never been so damn happy to be caught in a rainstorm in his life. A raindrop landed on the dip of her lip and clung there. He leaned over and licked it off with the tip of his tongue. Her skin tasted sweet and at the same time salty. Unable to stop there, he trailed the tip of his tongue down across her parted lips. Her breathing was shallow, warm against his face.

"I love . . . a good rain," she muttered against his lips.

"Me, too," he whispered.

Placing his hands on the curves of her waist, he proceeded to gently kiss droplets from her upper eyelids. She closed her eyes, inviting him to continue down. He kissed raindrops from her eyelashes, trailing kisses over her cheeks, the kisses growing more intense as he neared her mouth. Finally capturing her lips with his, he slipped his tongue into the warm moisture of her mouth, stroking her tongue. She returned his kiss, sweeping her hands up over his chest and shoulders, to the back of his neck, tunneling her fingers through his hair. He wrapped his arms around her, gathering up fistfuls of her camisole in his hands, pressing her body against him.

He drew back slightly, dropping his forehead against hers, gazing into her eyes, which peered up at him through slitted lids. "I lied," he said. "The other night wasn't a mistake. I want it to happen again." His heart pounded against his chest, his breathing becoming heavier. "Come home with me."

Holy shit. He'd never in his life invited a woman back to his place. He always went home with them. Would be kind of hard for him to bolt after sex if they were in *his* bed. Besides, he didn't want a woman in his home, snooping around his personal space.

She continued staring into his eyes, a hungry look filling hers. "I want to but—"

He brushed another kiss against her swollen lips. "No buts," he murmured, his lips still touching hers. His lips lingered, while he inhaled her warm breath, capturing it the moment she exhaled, sharing the same breath that had moments before filled her lungs. If they didn't share more than each other's breaths, and damn fast, he was gonna scoop her up in his arms, carry her over to his car, and take her in the back seat like some horny teenager. "You can't drive your scooter in this rain. I have to give you a ride somewhere." The word please hovered on the tip of his tongue, but he'd never begged a woman to sleep with him. He'd never had to. He glanced in the direction of the festival. "When in France, do as the French would. They're all about romantic liaisons."

"I suck at liaisons." Her breathing was coming in even faster, shallower, gasps, like it had the other night right before she'd orgasmed and let out a soft, erotic moan. "I . . . omigod, I want to."

"Then do it." He kissed her again, passionately, and she melted against him. He drew back slightly. "My car's right over there."

She slid a lazy gaze over to his Mercedes parked in the front row of the lot. The lustful haze in her eyes slowly gave way to panic. Her gaze narrowed and her teeth clamped down on her lower lip. She slipped her hands between their bodies, placing them against his chest, looking totally freaked out. She pushed him away. "I gotta go."

Confused by her sudden change in attitude, he stepped back, even though every muscle in his body tightened in protest and wanted to draw her against him. "I'll give you a ride home."

She shook her head vigorously. "That's okay, I don't live far." She turned and took off like a bat out of hell, as if hearing a starting gun fired at a race. As if she couldn't get away from him fast enough.

What the hell? He stood there watching her run away, fighting the urge to go after her. It was one thing he'd practically begged her to come home with him, he sure as shit wasn't chasing after her. Besides, she had a block head start.

He raked a frustrated hand through his hair, his gaze darting around, his mind searching for an explanation. He spied her purple shirt lying on the cement by the building's entry, under the awning. He walked over and picked it up. He raised it to his nose, inhaling the scent of cinnamon and something flowery. He took another whiff of it.

Get a friggin' grip! Next thing he knew he'd be whimpering like a puppy and scampering after her. He lowered the shirt, tightening his fingers around the material. No woman had ever caused him to act so irrationally and out of control before. To feel emotions so completely foreign they might as well be coming to him in Morse code for all he could decipher them. He was obsessed with Monica. When he wasn't close enough to physically touch her, inhale her scent, kiss her, he fantasized about doing it. He was fairly certain he'd even been dreaming about making love to her last night. When he hadn't been lying awake thinking about it.

He was so completely screwed.

Chapter Thirteen

The following morning, Monica removed the folder containing the plan for her next business venture from the bottom drawer of her desk. She tossed it in the garbage. No need for a backup plan. She was focusing all her energy on making this business as successful as Georgia and Mike's event. Reed's presence there had forced her to stay in control and to act confident, regardless of her feeling of impending doom. He was right, creativity couldn't be learned, it was a gift, one that she did indeed possess. Her back-up plans were merely proactive, enabling her to troubleshoot issues with confidence, which put a much more positive slant on it. She no longer felt like such a pessimist.

She opened the top drawer and removed the bottle of patchouli oil and the charm bag. She gave the bag a squeeze. She had four additional new clients from the Brewers game and eight from the newspaper article. One guy wanted to propose that weekend at Bastille Days. Nothing like planning ahead. The mime's skit would be perfect, but she needed to come up with something unique rather than using the rose and *je t'aime.*

A warm rush washed over her and the sound of Reed's I love you filled her head. His voice had been consumed with passion and feeling, his eyes brimming with sincerity. It hadn't been her imagination. The way he'd kissed her later in the rain, with an intense hunger, hadn't been her imagination either. Envisioning their bodies slick with rain, pressed against each other, nearly caused her to hyperventilate.

Leaving had seemed like the right thing to do at the time. When she'd glanced over at his car, at the license plate, *No Mer-ce*, she'd panicked. Her mind flashed back to the bet they'd made, to all their differences, to their talk about prenups. Yeah, maybe prenups weren't always a bad idea, since she'd never want to lose her business. Yet, if she did a prenup she felt like she'd be setting her marriage up to fail. Kind of like setting her business up to fail by having another business plan in the hopper.

But why had she really run away from him?

He'd asked her to come home with him. Maybe he invited women over all the time, and it meant nothing to him, but it meant a lot to her. Going home with him would have taken things to the next level. It wasn't like having spontaneous sex in a restaurant. It was the next step toward a relationship. A relationship that had no future. But couldn't she merely enjoy the present and the absolute best sex she'd ever experienced in her life? She hadn't had a fling since college. Maybe she was better at them now. Once Reed was gone, she wouldn't have the chance to find out. Since she was doing everything in her power to get rid of him, it was now or never.

She smacked her palm against her forehead repeatedly.

She was a total head case.

On the half hour run home, the more she'd thought about his license plate, the more she'd questioned its accuracy. Did it truly reflect Reed's attitude? Not only had he shown compassion by letting her plan an event for Georgia and Mike, he'd been pleased by the outcome. Maybe he was starting to show some mercy after all.

She tossed the patchouli oil back in the drawer and slammed it shut. She thunked her head against the desktop, her brain on overload, about to short circuit. She didn't have a clue what to think about Reed right now.

"As Time Goes By" sang out. She lifted her head from the desk and peered into the outer office at a tall, blond guy walking in. He spoke with Jordan a moment, then Jordan walked toward Monica's office, a look of ecstatic shock on her face, her eyes bugging out of her head.

"Do you know who that is?" Jordan jerked her head discreetly toward the outer office.

"Wild guess, a client?"

"Not *a* client, *the* client, *the* client of our freakin' lives. It's Chad Martin."

Monica glanced out at the guy perusing the posters on the walls. Not recognizing him, she gave Jordan a clueless stare.

Jordan rolled her eyes. "Get with the program, woman. No wonder you're still single. You have no idea who you should be going after. *Milwaukee Beat* named this guy one of the city's most eligible bachelors two years ago. He's a rich stockbroker. He didn't make the list the past two years because he's been dating the same chick for two years, *two* years. And now, he wants to marry her, and wants you, *you*," she pointed at Monica, "to plan the engagement proposal." When Jordan got excited, she had this annoying habit of repeating words.

"This could be huge," Monica muttered, trying not to leap from her chair with joy.

Jordan nodded, slapping a hand over her mouth, muffling a giddy squeal.

"This could be our biggest break of all. Think of the exposure we could get. Omigod, omigod." Monica took a calming breath, trying to contain her excitement, and not repeat herself. "Okay, let him in."

Jordan walked out then returned with Chad. Following introductions, Jordan left with a big grin on her face, and Chad sat in the chair across from Monica. He was blond, tan, muscular, handsome in an athletic sort of way. Understandable how he'd been voted one of the city's most eligible bachelors. However, unlike Reed, he didn't give her heart palpitations and induce an orgasm by merely being in the same room as her.

"So Chad, can I ask where you heard about my company?"

"Read the article in the paper."

She nodded. "Great, great." *Stop repeating yourself.* She tapped a pen nervously against the legal pad in front of her. *Stop tapping your pen.* She gripped the pen, poising it over the pad of paper.

"Why don't you tell me a bit about yourself and your girlfriend."

"Callie and I met on a cruise in the Mediterranean, in Portofino, Italy. It was nice, her not knowing who I was. After I was named most eligible bachelor that year I had women stalking me, going out of their way to set up 'chance' meetings. It was insane."

Hmm . . . kind of like Cynthia Reynolds.

A half hour later, Monica knew all of the couple's favorite hobbies, restaurants, plays, movies, vacation spots, etc. She promised to put together some ideas by the beginning of next week. He wanted to propose on the second anniversary of the date they'd met, at the end of the month. At least it gave her some time to create the perfect proposal.

Chad left and Jordan flew into the office. She perched on the edge of the chair across from Monica, bouncing up and down anxiously. "So what are you gonna do for him?"

"Not sure. I'll have to toss around some ideas. He wants to propose at the end of the month so I have a few weeks. He wants it to be intimate, yet have the whole city know about it."

Jordan's forehead scrunched up. "Gee, that's a bit of a challenge. Intimate, but have a half million people watching. But that's good. More exposure for you." Jordan fanned her hands out in front of her, envisioning the magnitude of the event. "Over a half million people watching . . . "

The pressure was on. Yes, this could be a huge boost to her company, but it could also go south real fast if things didn't come off without a hitch. It could make or break her company. This event had to be flawless.

She recalled Reed's little pep talk the day before. She was creative. She had the ability to troubleshoot anything that may go wrong. She was very good at what she did. Her business was going to succeed. She glanced at her computer monitor, void of sticky notes, which she'd input into her computer organizer. She was becoming more organized. Getting more clients . . .

She *could* do this.

"I don't think he necessarily wants people to be there watching him propose, but they should realize it's happened. That type of thing."

"That Brewers gig you did would have been perfect."

"Yeah, as far as having a large audience, but it wasn't really intimate and I couldn't see Chad dressing up in a foam bratwurst costume, participating in the sausage race, and proposing at the end of it."

"What's the budget?"

"Unlimited."

Jordan nodded in awe. "Good budget. So, if a gorgeous rich guy was going to propose to me, how would I want him to do it?" She stared off into space. "I know. I'd want him to take me to Tiffany's in Chicago for breakfast, then afterwards he'd let me pick out my own ring."

"They did that in the movie *Sweet Home Alabama.*"

"They didn't have breakfast and that's what they should have done. Like the movie. *Breakfast at Tiffany's.*"

"She never actually ate breakfast *in* Tiffany's."

"Technicality. You know what I mean."

"Besides, he wants it to be in Milwaukee and there's no Tiffany's here. And it has to be totally unique. I'm so not in tune with what the rich and famous would consider unique. These two vacation in Tahiti and the Greek Isles. They rented a private yacht in Monte Carlo and sailed the Mediterranean for a week. They jet off to New York City for a night to catch a Broadway show. They don't lead ordinary lives."

"Yeah, but you have a connection to the pampered affluent." Jordan pointed toward the wall, to Reed's office on the other side.

"Like he'd have a clue how to plan a romantic event."

Memories of their steamy kiss in the rain made her entire body cry out for Reed. Okay, Reed was way passionate. But passion didn't necessarily correlate with romance, love, and happily ever after. Besides, she couldn't face him after pushing him away. Talk about awkward.

"He just needs to be your lifeline to their way of thinking. Bounce ideas off him. He was one of this year's most eligible bachelors. He and Chad probably think alike. You never know, in two years you might be planning Reed's engagement proposal. So go ask him."

A sick feeling tossed Monica's stomach. No way would she be planning Reed's engagement proposal in another two years. No amount of media exposure or money would be worth seeing him ask another woman to marry him.

*

An hour later, Monica crumpled up a sheet of paper and tossed it onto a pile in the corner with the others. Every idea she came up with was too average. She planned unique events on a shoestring budget—you'd think she'd have no problem when the sky was the limit. But since the sky was the limit, this guy surely had some major expectations. Could she even meet, let alone exceed, his expectations here in Milwaukee? It's wasn't like she had a yacht in the Mediterranean to work with.

She dropped back in her chair, tossing the smiley face foam ball between her hands. The pressure of coming up with *wow* appeal was stifling her creativity. Usually, her mind was racing with ideas. She'd wake up in the morning and jot down ideas for events she'd dreamed about.

It wasn't that she'd lost the confidence she'd had earlier. She knew she was capable of executing a flawless event, she just had to come up with the event.

Jordan poked her head in the office. "How's it going?" She glanced over at the pile of crumpled up balls of paper. "Not so good, hey?"

"Everything they do together seems to somehow revolve around water and boats."

Jordan relaxed against the doorframe, a dreamy expression on her face. "How romantic is that?"

"They take his boat up to Door County on weekends. They went to the America's Cup once."

"Is that totally to die for or what?"

"Exactly. What can I do in Milwaukee that involves water that could outdo what they've done in the past?"

Jordan gazed off into space, then her eyes widened and inspiration took hold. "Okay, how about this?" She framed the air with her hands. "Picture Jacques Cousteau on a submarine and—"

"Isn't he dead?" Dumb question. Like that mattered to Jordan.

Jordan nodded faintly, brushing it off as a minor detail. She'd merely channel him and ask him to work the event.

"You could have a big fish swim by with a banner tied to its tail that reads *Will you marry me?* Or, Jacques Cousteau is French, and French is the language of love, maybe you could work that in somehow."

"No offense, but I don't wanna freak Chad out and lose his business by telling him some dead guy is hosting his event. Somehow I don't think he's the type who'd go for that."

Jordan shrugged. "People always say they want unique, but you give them unique and they freak out."

"Not to mention you'd never get me a gazillion feet under the lake in a submarine to execute the event."

"That's the problem. You're not a water person."

Monica had a near-death experience in her third grade swimming class and had steered clear of water ever since. She'd once done a cocktail cruise on the Milwaukee River, but the orange life jacket she'd insisted on wearing had clashed with her red sequined dress.

"You're having a hard time visualizing an event because you know squat about boating. You don't know what it feels like to be out on the high seas, the wind whipping in your hair, the water lapping the sides of the boat. Some sea air would do you good. Go down and walk around the marina, get inspired." Jordan slid her gaze toward the wall behind Monica. "He has a boat."

"How do you know that?"

"My friend has a sailboat we go out on once in a while. He pointed Reed's boat out to me. It's gimongous."

"I'm sure it is."

"So ask him to take you out. Seeing the city from the water would literally give you a different perspective on things."

"Just waltz in and ask him to take me sailing? I'm trying to get rid of his business, why would he want to help mine flourish?"

"Suck it up and ask Reed to see his boat. You want this to be the best event ever, don't you? Or I could start tweaking my Jacques Cousteau idea."

"Fine. I'll go talk to him."

Maybe Jordan was right. Although Monica wasn't about to ask Reed to take her sailing or to see his boat, she could pick his brain, without him knowing she was picking it. So it wouldn't look like she was coming to him for help.

"I got another piece of his mail this morning." Jordan flashed her a conspiratorial smile. "Haven't taken it over there yet. Maybe you should do that now."

They walked out to Jordan's desk where her friend handed her a postcard from Florence, Italy, with a collage of cafes, paintings, and old buildings on the front. "It's from some chick named Mandy, raving about the city being so romantic, he'd love it, she wished he was there, yaddah, yaddah, yaddah. Nothing too juicy. Except she's been sunbathing topless in Cannes."

Rather than scolding Jordan for reading his mail, she said, "Mandy," in a cutesy little voice. "Who sunbathes nude. Big surprise there."

Armed with the postcard and the best idea she had, Monica

headed over to Reed's. She stopped between their buildings, next to the lilac bush and flattened herself against the brick exterior. She read the postcard. The penmanship was small and precise, with a smiley face drawn in the "a" of Mandy. How cute. Jealousy consumed her and she glanced down at the lilac bush, fighting the urge to bury the postcard deep in the soil.

Who the hell was Mandy the topless sunbather? And if she wished Reed was there with her, why wasn't he?

Convincing herself that was none of her business, she stepped into the alcove of Reed's building, her hand poised over the door handle. Apprehension fluttered in her stomach. What if he was ticked off about her leaving him standing in the rain, horny and rejected with a bruised ego? What if he asked her to leave?

Even worse, what if he didn't give a rip she'd run off?

Her chest tightened and she feared a panic attack was coming on, but no stabbing pain followed. She hadn't had an attack in over four days. Since before she'd made love with Reed. Another reason for making love to Reed. It was a great stress reducer and good for her health. Although he'd been the one who'd brought on her first panic attack.

When she walked through the front door she was greeted by silence, no sounds of crying or screaming clients poured out from the inner office. That was a first.

Reed's office door was wide open and he glanced up from his desk, peering out as she approached. Their gazes locked. He didn't look upset or happy to see her. His expression was unreadable. She smoothed a nervous hand down her white cotton shirt, resting it on the waistband of her crisply pressed khaki scooter, trying to calm her nerves.

She took a deep breath and gave him a little finger wave. "Hi." She stopped in the doorway, waiting for him to invite her in, rather than barging in like every other time.

His faint smile didn't include his eyes, barely included his lips.

"Hi."

Silence filled the air. A more unnerving sound than the usual crying in his office. He still wasn't inviting her in. Not a good sign.

She raised the postcard in her hand, stepping inside his office. "Got another piece of your mail." She walked over to his desk and handed him the postcard.

Seeing the postcard brought a smile to his face, unlike Monica. Unable to wait, he flipped the card over and read it. His smile widened when he came to the ending, the part about Mandy sunbathing topless.

He set down the card and glanced up at her. "Sorry about that. I'll make sure the postman gets it together."

She smiled. "That's okay."

He appeared surprised by her reaction, which was much calmer than the last time she'd received his mail. Or more precisely, when she'd marched into his office with the divorce magazine, her wet cotton shirt and bra clinging to her breasts. Like they had been the night before in the rain. Both times he'd openly gawked at her breasts, and last night he'd looked ready to peel off her camisole and ravage them right there in public. She wished he had. Now, he wasn't even sneaking a peek at them.

His eyes reflected nothing and the smile the postcard had brought to his lips now faded. She wanted to see some emotion, preferably desire, passion, the longing to touch her the way her body ached to touch his. What if she stripped off her clothes and told him she regretted not going home with him? Would he take her right there on his desk or would he reject her, like she'd rejected him? Her stomach clenched at the thought of him pushing her away. Given the opportunity, she swore she'd never push him away again.

She gave him a subtle, flirtatious smile, stepping back from his desk, providing a better view of her bare legs, glad she'd worn a scooter. However, he didn't so much as glance at her legs.

She glared at the postcard on his desk. "So you have a friend in Florence?"

"My assistant. She and her husband took a two-week trip to the French and Italian Riviera and Tuscany."

A sense of relief swept over her and she tried not to let it reflect on her face. Mandy was his assistant, not a girlfriend. Although she sounded way too cute and perky to be his assistant. She'd expected his assistant to be some stuffy librarian type, serious and professional.

She scrambled to use the Riviera to segue into a conversation about boating. "Never been to the Riviera. Bet they have some expensive boats there." Duh.

He nodded, looking at her like she'd pulled that comment out of nowhere.

"It's nice living on a lake so at least we can hang out down by the water where it's cooler."

He nodded again. Not exactly a chatterbox today, was he?

"I'm actually going down to the lake tonight. Planning an engagement proposal for someone who loves boats so thought I'd swing by the marina and check it out." Client confidentiality prevented her from disclosing Chad's name. Reed likely knew him, or at least of him, both of them having boats and having been named one of Milwaukee's most eligible bachelors.

"You know security won't let you in the marina unless you're cleared by a boat owner there," he said.

Her gaze narrowed. Had Jordan left out that bit of info on purpose so Monica would have to rely on Reed to access the marina? Sneaky.

She glanced at the proposal in her hand, debating how to present the idea without directly asking for his opinion. On third thought, it certainly wasn't her best idea ever. Actually, she liked Jordan's Jacques Cousteau idea better. Scary.

His eyes softened slightly. "I'm gonna be down there working on my boat tonight," he said absently. "Dock K, slip eight. Check in at the registration station and tell security you're there to see me."

He wasn't exactly inviting her to pop by for a social visit, merely allowing her to use his name to gain access to the marina. Did he want her to stop by and see him?

"Maybe I'll see ya down there." She hesitated then turned to leave.

"I have your shirt."

She turned back toward him. "What shirt?"

He pulled a plastic bag from his bottom drawer and handed it to her. She peaked inside to find the purple shirt she'd left lying on the cement last night. It was a good sign he'd taken it rather than leaving it there. She peered over at Reed to confirm that theory. Rather than eying the shirt, thinking about their kiss like she was, his gaze was glued to a file on his desk. Lovely. A cold, boring legal document held his interest more than she did.

"Thanks," she muttered, then turned and left.

*

Reed watched Monica walk out of his office, his gaze fixed on the back of her slender thighs, recalling the smooth feel of her skin. His gaze traveled up, watching the slight swing to her ass, hidden beneath the loose fitting skirt. He imagined the rounded curves of her butt and the satiny feel of her thong. Or maybe it was a lace one today. He'd wanted to strip off her skirt and find out for himself.

It'd taken every ounce of restraint he had to not so much as glance at her legs, her breasts, or the sexy dip over her lip. One glance at her breasts and he'd have lost it like he had last night in the rain. Screw asking her back to his house, he'd have taken her right there in his office. Or rather, he'd have wanted to but she'd likely have rejected him once again. Sounded arrogant, but he couldn't remember the last time a woman had said no. And of all the women to do it, it had to be Monica. The one woman he craved more than any other.

Monica walked out the front door and he dropped back against the chair, letting out a frustrated groan. He had to get over his obsession with that woman. Returning her shirt was a start. He'd been taking it out of the drawer every five minutes and sniffing it like some hound dog picking up the scent of a fox.

Monica was a *total* fox.

He glanced down at the drawer where the scent of cinnamon likely lingered. Get a friggin' grip! No way in hell was he opening that drawer. He clenched his hand into a fist and slammed it down resolutely on his desk.

He hadn't even planned on hanging out on his boat tonight. Yet, inviting her on his boat was a step back from inviting her to his house. He could review Natalie's file on the boat. She'd dropped off his dad's personal tax returns for the past three years, financial statements, and real estate holdings. His father's lawyer hadn't yet responded to his request for his father's corporate tax returns for the past few years. His father could afford to be an ass and play games, but he couldn't avoid handing them over forever. Or avoid the inevitable jail sentence for tax evasion if Reed opted to take that route.

Either way, the man was screwed.

Chapter Fourteen

Sea-Duction. Monica read the name painted in flaming red letters on the back of a boat. Underneath, in smaller print, it read *Seazzling Hot.* A twenty-something blond chick in a size two leopard print thong bikini sat on the back deck with her sugar daddy—a graying guy who was quite buff, in his mid-forties.

Monica continued down the cement walk, glancing around at the *boatload* of money parked in the marina and dotting the lakefront. Unbelievable. She couldn't afford a car, let alone a boat. One more thing she and Reed didn't have in common.

As she approached slip K, she zoned in on a man sitting at a table on the back deck of a boat. Reed. Her internal radar could pick up his signal if they were ten miles offshore in the middle of a dense fog. Her heart raced and all her senses were heightened, on red alert.

She tugged down the bottom of her low-cut, royal blue spandex halter top, making sure the top of her breasts were visible, along with a glimpse of her white lace bra. She'd worn the shortest white skirt she had to reveal as much skin as possible, and red wedge sandals to make her legs appear longer and more slender. It was also the most nautical outfit she owned.

He'd damn well better notice her body in this.

She peered over at Betty Boop painted on the back of Reed's boat. Was Betty the name of an old flame? She couldn't imagine Reed being a fan of the cartoon character. She doubted he'd even watched cartoons as a kid. Not surprisingly, the boat was a sleek, white yacht, at least sixty feet long. And it was parked at the very end of the wooden dock, a gazillion miles from shore, in deep water.

Her heart thumped in her chest, causing the pulse in her ears to throb. Taking a motivating breath, she gave herself a little pep talk. She could do this. Not like she was going to trip and fall in the water. Right? She turned and walked down the middle of the wooden dock toward Reed's boat. She focused on admiring the boats, rather than the water getting deeper the further out she walked. When she reached Reed's boat at the end, her entire body was sweating bullets. She wiped perspiration from her forehead and prayed for rain, wanting some relief, and to replay the night before but with a different ending.

Unfortunately, there wasn't a cloud in sight.

Reed was engrossed in paperwork spread out on the table in front of him. He had on a white T-shirt and jeans. She walked down the dock alongside the boat.

"Hi," she said.

He glanced up. "Hey . . . " his voice trailed off as his gaze headed south, traveling down over her breasts to her legs. His intense gaze lingered on her thighs and she wondered if, like herself, he was envisioning her legs wrapping securely around his waist, drawing his naked body toward hers while she'd laid on the red cushions.

Mission accomplished. The outfit had done its job.

As if suddenly aware he was staring, his gaze shot up and met hers. He stepped over to the side of the boat. She eyed the white T-shirt stretched across his broad chest, her fingers flexing, itching to rip it off his body.

He offered his hand to help her aboard. "There's a step on the inside, right there." He gestured down to it.

She reached out and took his hand. A warm, safe, secure feeling instantly wrapped around her. It wasn't just about Reed keeping her from falling in the water, but a deeper sense of protection, like he wouldn't let anything harm her. Yet, she peered cautiously over the side of the boat, gaze glued to the glaring gap of water between the dock and the boat. A foot max, but it seemed to get wider the longer she stared at it.

He gave her hand a reassuring squeeze. "You won't fall."

She put a death grip on his hand, avoiding looking down at the water as she lifted her leg over the side of the boat. She planted a foot firmly on the step then lifted the other one over and onto the wooden deck. Losing her balance and falling against Reed would be an excuse to press her body against his, but a tad too obvious.

She slid onto a wooden chair at the table, stealing Reed's seat. She felt safer facing the high-rise condos jutting up from the hill overlooking the lake than the large expanse of open water with no sight of the Michigan shoreline on the other side. She lounged back in the chair, crossing her legs, allowing a clear view of the tops of her thighs.

Reed closed the file in front of her and slid it to the other side of the table. "I was just about to open a bottle of wine. Would you like a glass? Or I could make Bellinis. We never got that glass of champagne last night."

"A Bellini would be nice."

She wasn't sure what exactly a Bellini was, but anything made with champagne couldn't be bad. He walked up a few steps and headed inside the boat. Her gaze followed him through the cabin, past shiny wood cabinets accented with brass and a cream leather bench seat wrapped around a wooden table. He disappeared down a set of stairs at the front next to the captain's seat. She tried to ignore the gentle rocking of the boat, and the fact she had no clue where the lifejackets were stored. Instead, she focused on her purpose for being there. To get a feel for boating, to become inspired, to get rid of her creative block.

To seduce Reed.

Reed returned a few minutes later with two flutes of champagne. He handed her one then sat on the chair across from her. She took a gulp of champagne, savoring the peachy taste as the bubbles floated to the top of the glass. She had the sensation they were floating up from her stomach into her chest and blamed the champagne for her nervous jitters rather than Reed's close proximity.

She rested her hands just beneath her breasts, lacing her fingers together. Her action succeeded in drawing his gaze right where she wanted it.

She glanced around nonchalantly. "So, where do you keep the life vests?"

He pointed to a cream cushioned bench seat running the length of the back of the boat. "Under there. Why, wanna take the boat out?"

She shook her head vigorously—a bit too vigorously. Relax. Stay calm. In control. "Just curious. Always good to be prepared in case of an emergency." She laughed, a forced, nervous laugh.

He gave her a curious stare and she took another gulp of champagne.

"How long you had this boat?"

"It's actually a buddy's of mine. He moved to Arizona. Not a lot of need for a boat there. I'm boat sitting until he sells it. Been debating buying it myself. Getting kind of attached to it. It's a great way to get away from everything. Out on the water with nobody around."

Please don't buy it. She could never spend weekends out on his boat or take trips up to Door County like Chad Martin and his girlfriend. She'd have to admit being afraid of the water and unable to swim.

Since when would they be spending their weekends together?

Besides the fact they weren't dating, they both worked weekends. She doubted Reed took time off work for a leisurely boat ride up to Door County. And events would soon be consuming her entire weekends, with no time or energy in between for dating. Another reason they could never have a relationship. It had taken thirteen failed business ventures to get to this point. She wasn't going to blow it by being distracted with a relationship that had no future. A brief fling, however, wouldn't be distracting.

She peered off at the cityscape. "Bet it's romantic out on the water at night with the city all lit up . . . " she trailed off, picturing the romantic setting, letting out a contented sigh.

"It's an awesome view," Reed said.

She glanced over at him and their gazes locked. It wasn't the city's view he was admiring. She swallowed hard. "I was telling you about my client who's into boats and planning to propose," she explained.

He nodded, his thumb gently stroking the stem of his flute. Warm tingles concentrated between her upper thighs. That smug expression told her he knew perfectly well she was turned on by his thumb. Her body temp kicked up a notch as Monica decided this was a game for two. She slowly raised her champagne flute to her mouth. He watched her lips hug the rim of the glass and take a leisurely sip. His gaze still glued to her mouth, she lowered the glass and swiped her tongue over her lips. She was certain she heard his breath hitch in his throat as he looked away.

"I'm still tweaking the proposal, trying to decide on the best way for him to propose."

Reed nodded slowly, gazing out at the water behind her. "If I were him, I'd take her out on my boat at dusk before the whole city lights up against the evening sky. Just the two of us with an occasional seagull gliding overhead, looking back at the city. I'd have taken the boat out the night prior to make sure I had it timed to a tee. We'd enjoy a glass of wine as the city lights flickered on."

Her gaze fixed on Reed's rather than the cityscape, envisioning the setting through his eyes, which glimmered with inspired enthusiasm.

"It would be a bottle of Bordeaux, one from the region of France we'd visited the summer before, on our first trip away together. I'd have 'You Light Up my Life' playing on CD . . . " He glanced away from the water and over at her, a smile curling the corners of his mouth and crinkling the corners of his eyes. "I'm kidding about the song. I'm not that hokey."

Monica merely nodded, the Debby Boone song playing in her head.

"The song would be something vintage, with staying power, like our relationship. Maybe a Sinatra tune."

"'The Way You Look Tonight.'"

He nodded.

Did he remember she'd been singing that the first time they'd met?

He straightened in his chair, leaning toward her, resting his elbows against the table. "Then as the city lit up," he gazed deep into her eyes, "I'd turn to her with my grandmother's ring in a black velvet box," he opened an imaginary box in her direction, "and say 'this ring brought my grandparents fifty-four years of happiness. I want it to do the same for us. Will you marry me?'" His voice lowered to a soft whisper.

He gazed expectantly at her, as if waiting for a response. She leaned in toward him, the word *yes* playing on the tip of her tongue. She swallowed hard, staring into his eyes. Her body was on fire, a combination of the Bellini and Reed's proposal. Last night he'd said I love you and tonight he was proposing. He sounded like he'd been planning the proposal forever. And his grandmother's ring was so romantic. She wanted to hold out her hand and feel him slipping the ring—imaginary or not—on her finger. Goose bumps skittered across her finger, up her arm, and over her entire body.

"What does the ring look like?" She wanted to envision the entire scene right down to every detail.

"It's platinum with a half carat diamond."

Not only was she impressed he knew what his grandmother's ring looked like, but the ring was quite modest compared to the three-carat diamond she'd figured he'd buy a woman. It was way more sentimental and romantic.

"Sounds perfect," she muttered. She stroked a fingertip over her bare ring finger, picturing his grandmother's ring there. She peered over to find him studying her finger.

"Her fingers were thin like yours," he said.

She suddenly felt like she was in over her head, drowning, in need of an emotional lifejacket. Deciding to have a fling with Reed was one thing. Wearing his grandmother's ring another. It would never happen. She needed to squelch any fantasies otherwise. She tried to shove the thoughts from her head, but glanced back down at her ring finger.

"Thought you said you weren't creative."

He shrugged, relaxing back in his chair. "That's not real creative."

Maybe it wasn't hugely creative, but it was totally romantic.

"Being on this boat at night is one of my favorite spots, so it was a no-brainer this is where I'd propose."

As if on cue, lights began flickering on, the cityscape coming to life, adding to the romantic ambiance. Lovely.

"Maybe Chad Martin could propose—" she slapped a hand over her mouth. Damn champagne. "Shit," she muttered. "You can't tell a soul he's going to propose."

A reassuring smile curled the corners of Reed's lips. "Don't worry, I won't."

"Do you know him?"

"He has a boat here in the marina so I see him around once in a while."

"What I was going to say is he's been everywhere and done everything. I think maybe he needs something a little more showy. He seems like the showy type. Not real low key."

"Yeah, he would." Reed stared into his champagne flute, a pensive look on his face, then he peered over at her. "I know a guy in Chicago who owns a tall ship. Maybe you could rent it."

"Is that one of the ships with the tall sails?"

He nodded. "It's a kick-ass boat. Made in Italy."

Monica's eyes widened. "Chad and his girlfriend met in Italy. Their favorite restaurant is De Luca's. I could have the chef prepare their favorite meal onboard. Have their favorite wine from Italy. And their favorite waiter serve it. Have lights along the boardwalk or on a building light up that read *Will You Marry Me Callie?* Would that be showy enough?"

Reed nodded. "He's lucky he's got you planning this for him."

She collapsed back in her chair. The pressure was off.

This was an awesome idea and it had partly been Reed's. She was blown away that he was capable of creating such a romantic proposal. It caused even more doubt that his *No Mer-ce* license plate accurately described him and gave her even more delusional hope that they could have a relationship.

She wiped perspiration from her upper lip, drawing Reed's attention to her mouth. She needed to cool down and jumping in the lake wasn't an option. She popped up from her chair. "Can I use your bathroom?"

"Ah, sure. Head down the stairs at the front and go all the way back. There's a bathroom in the master bedroom."

The master bedroom?

She bolted inside the cabin, inhaling the scent of lemon furniture polish and leather, then headed down the stairs past a galley done in black and stainless steel. She walked to the end of the short, narrow, hallway and into the bedroom. A queen size bed covered with a tan duvet occupied most of the room. Spotting a few photos on the nightstand, she walked over and picked up a photo of Reed and his mother along with some older man. An ex-boyfriend of Lila's maybe? Big smiles on their faces, they appeared to be sitting in a bar drinking, bottles of beer raised high in the air.

"'Whiskey You're the Devil,'" Reed said.

Almost dropping the picture frame, her gaze darted over to him. He didn't appear upset, but she promptly set the frame down on the table. Standing in the narrow doorway, he looked even taller, his shoulders even broader.

"Sorry. Didn't mean to be nosey."

A reminiscent expression brought a smile to his lips and a sparkle to his blue eyes. He nodded toward the photo. "Took my mother to Ireland last summer for two weeks. Her grandmother was from there. She discovered a cousin through genealogy research. That's him in the photo, he owns a pub. We spent a fair amount of time there with locals. 'Whiskey You're the Devil' was the song we were singing. Still remember the words."

Her gaze narrowed in doubt, unable to picture Reed participating in a pub sing-along.

"Whiskey you're the devil," he began singing a catchy little tune and she stared at him in shock. "Leadin' me astray, o'er hills and mountains, and to Amerikay, you're sweeter, stronger, decenter, spunkier than tea . . . " he trailed off, apparently noticing the stunned expression on her face. "Was a good time."

He had a great voice, whereas Monica was completely tone deaf—but she'd kill to hang out in a pub with him singing songs. To discover more of this fun-loving side he kept so well hidden. A quality she sought in a man and had documented in the letter to her soul mate.

She walked around the side of the bed and stopped at the foot of it, the backs of her legs brushing against the soft duvet, only a few feet between the end of the bed and the door. Reed stepped aside to let her through. Not a good sign.

She gazed over at him from beneath her lashes, giving him a seductive pout a French woman would envy, and any sane man would hopefully ravage. "Does your offer still stand?"

"What offer's that?" From the raspy, oozing with sex appeal tone of his voice, he knew exactly what offer.

"This isn't your house, but it's close to it." She glanced suggestively over her shoulder at the bed then slowly slid her gaze back to him.

He stepped toward her, stopping just inches in front of her, peering down at her with a smoldering gaze. "Offer still stands."

She skimmed her hands up over his abs, fanning them across his chest. She placed a kiss to his chest, exhaling a warm breath, letting her lips linger, feeling his heart pounding against them. Cupping her cheeks and gently tilting her face toward his, he stopped just shy of kissing her.

"Should we christen my boat?"

His admission of never having had a woman in this bed nearly made her orgasm. She curled her fingers into the front of his T-shirt, aching to get at his chest beneath. "Aye, aye, captain."

She captured his mouth with hers, thrusting her tongue inside, setting the tone for their lovemaking to come. No way were they taking it slow and easy like the last time. His hands were all over her, his tongue doing a wild tango with hers, telling her they were on the same page.

She slipped her tongue from his mouth, their lips still touching. "I want you now." Her voice was breathless, her breathing ragged as she tugged the bottom of his shirt from his jeans. "Can't wait."

"Then don't," he said, stripping off his shirt.

She undid his jeans' button and zipper. Before she could free him of his pants, he peeled off her shirt then her bra. He pulled off his pants, then slipped his hands under her arms, drawing her toward him while easing back on the bed. He peered up at her, a seductive smile curling the corners of his mouth. She smiled back.

He reached over and grabbed a condom out of the nightstand. "Sorry, I'm out of green ones." He arched a brow. "But I still feel lucky."

She nodded. Oh, yeah.

He sheathed his erection then slid up over her, their bodies touching. He gazed deep into her eyes, the raw hunger in his grew even more intense. He placed warm kisses along her collarbone while positioning his erection between her legs. They held each other's gaze as he slowly slipped inside her, her breath catching in her throat, her lids becoming heavy.

He slid almost all the way out and waited a taunting moment before thrusting back inside her, harder, deeper, causing her back to arch and a moan to escape up her throat.

Their gazes locked, she wrapped her legs possessively around his waist, pressing her heels into the small of his back, attempting to aid him in plunging even deeper inside her. No matter how deep he went, it couldn't be deep enough. She wanted him to fill her inside. She grazed her nails down his back as each thrust grew more intense, more powerful.

Both physically and emotionally, she was a goner.

Chapter Fifteen

The following morning Monica and Hope walked in the back door of K & H Steakhouse. Monica had only eaten at their restaurant once, a few years ago for Hope's parents' anniversary party. The food was good, but the place resembled a stodgy mens-only club with dark walls and deep mahogany furnishings. However, the kitchen was bright and airy with white walls and lots of shiny stainless steel. They were boxing up the pastry tools and utensils when Kyle came in to open. He looked even scarier than he had a few days ago. Seemed *Wild Man of Borneo* had contracted jungle fever with dark circles under his eyes, red blotches on his face covered in a white crusty cream, and he was wheezing like a four-pack-a-day smoker in need of oxygen.

He eyed the half dozen cardboard boxes on the floor. "What the hell are you doing?" He glanced over at Hope, gaze narrowing, jaw dropping. Rather than having on one of her typical long flowing floral sundresses, she'd borrowed Monica's hot pink spandex mini dress that accentuated curves typically hidden by loose fitting garments. Hope had wanted to show Kyle what he was missing. And from the shocked expression on his face, his bloodshot eyes hadn't impaired his vision.

"Picking up a few things for my new business," Hope said, dropping a wire whisk into a box.

"You can't just come in here and . . . " Kyle stopped ogling her breasts, "what business?"

"I'm opening a pastry shop. Movers are coming by to take one of the ovens, along with the espresso, cappuccino, and coffeemakers. Oh, and the tea urns."

Major lie. There were no movers, because there was no business.

Yet. Monica knew Hope hadn't decided what she wanted to do, but she was freakin' out that she wouldn't find a full-time job and she needed money, so she was bluffing. Not only was she becoming more assertive, she was becoming very good at playing games with Kyle's mind. Monica was rubbing off on her.

"You don't determine the division of assets, a judge does."

He wiped the perspiration from his forehead. "Jesus, it's like a sauna in here."

"It's like a meat locker in here," Hope said. "You look like crap."

"Haven't been sleeping well."

"Been sleeping alone though I bet," Monica quipped.

He shot her a pissed-off glare.

"Hmm," Monica mused, giving him a speculative look.

"It's not your damn spell," Kyle snapped. "There's some sort of flu going around."

"Right," Monica said, studying his face.

The spell was definitely working. No way could women find Kyle attractive. Fear of contracting something would keep them away if nothing else.

A guy strolled in the back door, dressed in pair of faded jeans and a black Harley Davidson T-shirt. Harrison Bradley, the head chef. The restaurant owed much of its success to the renowned chef with thick black hair and dreamy brown eyes. Even women who were die-hard vegetarians patronized the steakhouse, hoping he might serve them breakfast in bed.

Hope glanced at her reflection in a copper pot hanging over the counter, discreetly foofing her hair.

Harrison peered over at her, quirking a surprised brow, an interested smile on his face as he took in her new look. "Hey, Hope."

"Hey." She gave him a coquettish smile.

Omigod. If Hope started dating Kyle's head chef, that would kill him faster than the flesh eating disease.

Harrison handed Kyle an envelope. "My mother's sick, I gotta head back to New York."

Kyle eyed the envelope. "What's this?"

"My notice."

Kyle's eyes shot open, capillaries about bursting. "Your notice? When are you leaving?"

"Tomorrow."

"Tomorrow!" Kyle braced a hand on the stainless steel counter, steadying himself.

Harrison shrugged. "Sorry. Tonight will be my last night." He gestured toward the envelope. "I included a list of possible replacements."

"Why don't you just take a week off?"

"It'll probably take a few months. Victor can handle things until you find a replacement."

Kyle shook his head frantically. "Victor doesn't have the experience to be head chef."

"Sorry. Been thinking about leaving here anyway." Harrison glanced over at Hope, giving her a sexy little smile and she blushed. If Kyle hadn't been on the verge of a stroke, he'd likely have noticed the sexual tension between his wife and his employee. "See ya around." That sounded like a definite promise. He nodded goodbye to Hope and strolled out.

Kyle clutched the envelope, gasping as if on his last breath. His gaze darted to Monica. "Take . . . this . . . effing," he sputtered, "spell . . . off . . . me."

Monica gave him a baffled look. "Thought you didn't believe in spells?"

Kyle snarled. "Just do it." He glanced at the boxes on the floor, then at Hope. "Leave this shit. I'll sell my Harley and have the money to you within a week."

Abracadabra. The spell was removed and Kyle was suddenly looking much more attractive. At least financially.

Chapter Sixteen

Reed grabbed his briefcase and headed out of his office, on his way to a hearing, another deadbeat dad in contempt of the court's temporary order to pay the required child support. It would be all Reed could do not to knock the guy flat on his ass in front of the judge.

As he walked toward the front door, a woman entered. Mid-thirties, petite, dressed in a navy pantsuit, she looked quite put together, except for the lost look on her face. He'd seen the same expression a thousand times. She was looking to Reed for direction. To help her chart a new course for her future, to navigate the divorce process.

"Can I help you?" he asked.

"Are you Reed Walker?"

He nodded. "What can I do for you?"

"I'd like to hire your services. I'm getting," she swallowed hard, her gaze narrowing, "a divorce."

"I'm sorry, I was just heading out. I'd be happy to set up an appointment for an initial consultation."

"Oh." She nodded absently, looking even more lost. "Of course. I should have called first."

He glanced at his watch. He could give her a few minutes. "Come into my office and I'll check my schedule."

She introduced herself as Vicky and he led her back to his office. She took a seat in front of his desk and he remained standing. He removed his BlackBerry from his waist. He scrolled through his schedule to find every day, including weekends, jam packed with appointments and court dates. An initial consultation lasted about an hour. He charged a hundred and fifty bucks, half his hourly rate. Many lawyers didn't charge a fee, but charging helped weed out people who were merely flirting with the idea of a divorce and not committed to it.

He wasn't the most expensive lawyer in the city, nor the cheapest. He only represented the underdog clients, usually women, and the underdog generally couldn't afford a divorce. Although often times he got the court to mandate the spouse pay his fees depending on his client's financial resources and the facts of the case. His reputation kept him busy as hell and his ability to wrap up cases quickly enabled him to handle numerous clients at once.

"I could squeeze you in next Tuesday at ten. Would that work?"

She nodded, massaging a nervous hand over her neck.

"This will be a preliminary meeting, to get to know each other. I'll explain the divorce process, costs, etc. The fee is a hundred and fifty dollars for the consultation."

She nodded okay.

"Have either of you petitioned for divorce yet?"

She shook her head, fidgeting with the wedding ring on her finger. A simple gold band, no diamond.

"It would have been our tenth anniversary next week," she said, staring at her ring. "Well, I guess it still will be since we're still married. Roger—" A sob caught in her throat, and her body went rigid as she forced it back down and appeared to desperately maintain her composure.

"Have you two been through marriage counseling? Any chance of a reconciliation?" He immediately regretted the question, since it could open a floodgate of emotions he didn't have time to deal with right now. So why had he felt compelled to ask it rather than at the initial consultation?

She shook her head. "He would never agree to marriage counseling. He doesn't have the time. He's married to his job. He's paid more attention to me since I moved out two weeks ago than he has in years. But I doubt he'll ever change." She glanced over at Reed, as if seeking his opinion, as if he knew this Roger guy. She sounded like she hoped he could change. Was she merely hoping to give this guy a wakeup call?

"Are you sure you're ready to move forward with the divorce?" What the hell? She'd just said there was no chance of reconciliation. Move on.

She nodded faintly, sliding her ring around on her finger.

Were woman usually still wearing their wedding rings when they came into his office? No clue. He remembered one time when he'd told a woman her husband wanted the value of the ring included in their settlement, she'd taken the ring from her purse, set it on his desk, and pummeled the shit out of it with his paperweight. She'd succeeded at destroying several manicured nails, not the diamond.

He thought back to Georgia and Mike. What if Monica hadn't intervened and she'd gone through with the divorce, only to later regret it?

Christ, what was his deal? He'd never had the time or desire for emotional bullshit before. Monica was making him sappy. If he didn't get his act together, he was going to destroy his reputation as a pit bull divorce lawyer.

"Okay then, I'll see you next week."

Vicky went to stand and broke down crying, collapsing back onto the chair. Shit. He handed her a tissue and started giving her his usual pep talk. That she wasn't the loser her husband was, that she'd succeed while he failed, blah, blah, blah. He wondered if the words had always sounded as cold and meaningless to his clients as they did to him right now.

If his pep talk didn't get them to stop crying, he generally gave them five minutes to get it out of their system before handing them over to Mandy. He glanced helplessly out at Mandy's empty desk. He wanted to deal with the facts, the legal process, not the emotions. Mandy usually dealt with clients who were outside his emotional comfort zone and referred them to a therapist. He placed an awkward hand on Vicky's shoulder, something he never did. Maintaining a physical distance helped him maintain an emotional one also.

He snapped his hand away as if he'd touched a hot burner.

What was he supposed to do? He couldn't shove her out the door while she was bawling her eyes out.

"I'll be right back."

He marched out and headed over to Monica's office. His gaze darted around at posters of classic romance movies. The place reeked like flowers, but there were none in sight. Jordan sat at a desk in the outer office, wearing a goofy-ass grin.

What was up with her?

"That proposal you helped Monica with was the sweetest ever. I couldn't believe it."

Monica was turning him into a chick, planning romantic events! He'd never even thought about how he'd propose to a woman because he'd never planned on doing it. The idea had come out of nowhere. His grandmother's ring was unpretentious and not the least bit flashy, like Monica. Not that he planned on giving it to her. It just reminded him of her . . . shit.

"Ah, yeah, thanks," he said, brushing off her comment. He marched past, spotting Monica through a glass paned window in an inner office.

When he entered her office, Monica popped up from her desk, looking surprised, yet happy to see him. The hemline of her short pink skirt flirted with the tops of her thighs where he'd placed kisses the night before, and her white shirt molded her breasts like his hands had.

She needed to dress more professionally, damnit.

He forced his gaze away, inhaling the scent of cinnamon.

Not only did he lose control when he was around Monica, he feared he was losing his edge, and would ultimately lose the career he'd worked a lifetime to build. He slid his gaze from the *Sabrina* movie poster on the wall to the direction of his office where Vicky sat bawling. He knew damn well they had no future. They were too opposite. Despite the fact that Monica made him feel unlike any woman ever had, he wasn't about to throw away his career on a fling.

Monica stepped around her desk, toward him. He bolted to the other side of the room. He glanced over at her, noticing the confused and wounded expression on her face. He felt like a total ass after they'd spent hours making love the night before and she'd moaned out his name as she'd come, not merely the first, but also the second time.

He shoved the thoughts aside.

This was professional, not personal. Bullshit. The problem was they'd gotten too personal professionally.

He glanced into the outer office where Jordan sat at her desk staring at him, still wearing that goofy-ass grin. He peered over at Monica's desk, focusing on the foam smiley face. "I have to go to court and can't get this client out of my office. She's a complete basket case. I don't have time to deal with her. Thought maybe you could talk to her."

"Ah, yeah, sure."

Walking over to her, he slipped a keychain from his pocket and removed the office key. He held the key out to her, avoiding her gaze. "Please lock up when you're done."

She nodded, taking the key. "Not a problem."

He shot her a fleeting glance. The hurt look in her eyes made him want to kick his own ass. As much as he wanted to reach out and touch her, he couldn't. Things were already way too complicated. "Thanks." He turned and marched out, as if evacuating a building of weeping women.

Even if this Vicky woman didn't turn out to be the second relationship Monica saved, he needed to be gone, and fast. Forget the fact his new office wouldn't be finished for a month.

Better to be a lawyer without an office than a lawyer without any cojones.

*

After a half hour of consoling Vicky, Monica was mentally spent. She didn't know how Reed dealt with emotionally distraught clients on a daily basis. Her clients were upbeat and optimistic, yet her job still a bit stressful. No wonder his job had made him negative and cynical, listening to people whine about spouses all day long. It would have sucked the life out of her by now.

Vicky had decided to seek counseling and get her emotions in check before returning to Reed's office. Although emotional and confused, she seemed quite dissatisfied with her marriage. Monica wasn't comfortable trying to solve their problems with a romantic event. Vicky's problems ran deeper. If Vicky turned out to be the second client whose marriage she helped save, that meant one more couple and Reed would be gone.

The thought of Reed moving away caused an overwhelming sense of loss and emptiness inside her. Although she wondered if it bothered him. Sure, he'd had to get to court earlier, but he hadn't even looked at her when he was in her office. Like making love for hours the night before had meant nothing to him. That he didn't even care to continue their "fling" when she knew it was much more than that for both of them. She'd had sex with guys who were just in it for the sex. She could tell by the way Reed touched her, looked at her, this was about more. Once again, it was like he was a different person when at work. He'd sounded calloused about Vicky, but she was certain she'd seen a hint of compassion in his eyes. Or was it merely her imagination, the imagination that had convinced her Reed had feelings for her?

Jordan was at lunch when "As Time Goes By" sang out. Monica peered into the outer office to find Lila, Reed's mother. She gave Monica a bright smile and wave before proceeding into her office, a definite bounce in her step.

Please do not let her have another event in mind for Reed. Monica couldn't bring herself to set him up with another old flame. No way, no how.

Lila entered the office. "What a simply lovely day." She relaxed into the chair across from Monica. "Reed's office is closed. Must be in court, so I thought I'd pop over and say hello. Wasn't that French festival fun? We sat at a little makeshift sidewalk café and listened to the accordion player for hours. It was so romantic. The perfect spot for lovers. Don't you think?" She wore a hopeful expression, and Monica felt like she was being pumped for info on her and Reed's relationship.

Monica told Lila about Georgia and Mike's event, reinforcing she and Reed had been there together solely for business. Although that had changed before the end of the evening with a steamy kiss in the rain.

"Reed absolutely adores Paris. He'd be the perfect travel companion. He knows all the restaurants and places to go. He speaks French, and knows art. Boy, does he know his art." She opened her mouth to continue, but snapped it shut, looking mildly embarrassed, undoubtedly realizing she was laying it on a bit thick. "I have to apologize again for putting you in that awkward position with Ms. Reynolds. I had no idea the woman has bats in her belfry. I assure you, Reed has had plenty of sane girlfriends. That woman who filed the paternity suit against him knew exactly what she was doing, she was merely desperate."

Paternity suit? When Reed had mentioned that at the Casbah she'd been in the midst of a meltdown and had forgotten all about it.

"It wasn't his child. He had a DNA test. I don't understand with all the testing available nowadays why a woman would lie about such a thing. Desperation I guess. He's quite the catch. If the child had been his, he certainly would have done the right thing. He would never turn away his own child. Not like his father . . . " she trailed off, obviously having said too much.

Reed's father had abandoned him?

"We had so much fun at Bastille Days, we went back again last night." Lila reverted back to a safer topic. "Drank some champagne and ate these strawberries covered with chocolate that looked like little tuxedo jackets."

"Bill seems like a nice guy."

Lila's expression turned dreamy. "He is. Honestly, that's one of the reasons I came to see you. I'd like you to plan our wedding reception."

"I'm honored, but I'm not really a wedding planner per se. I do more intimate romantic events than parties. Reed mentioned you were getting married. Sounds like you've set a date."

Lila glanced past Monica at the common wall to Reed's office. "Well," she lowered her voice, "we're actually already married." Her face lit up. "Got married on Tuesday. Going to Bastille Days was a romantic end to the day."

Monica's eyes about bugged out of her head. Holy crap. Did Reed know this? Probably not with Lila's hushed tone. He'd go berserk that she'd gotten married without telling him and that she hadn't signed a prenup. Reed should have been open with her before about this guy's divorces. Lila appeared to truly love Bill. Hopefully, he loved her as much.

"Congratulations," she finally managed. She glanced down at the woman's ring-less finger.

"Don't say anything. I plan to tell Reed at the party next weekend."

Great. Now Monica knew Reed's mother had gotten married before he did. She couldn't keep this a secret when she wanted an open and honest relationship with him. She'd had no qualms going behind his back before, but a lot had changed since then. And last time she and Lila had conspired together against Reed it hadn't turned out well. Except for the fact they'd made love of course.

"I know it's none of my business, but after the Cynthia Reynolds event, I'd hate to plan another one with any nasty surprises. I mean, don't you think he'll be upset finding this out at the party and not beforehand?"

"If he'd known about the wedding, he'd have shown up at the courthouse with a prenup and put a damper on my wedding day."

She looked saddened not having his support. "So I thought maybe if he sees us at the party and how happy we are he'd be happy for me. Guess I also figured he wouldn't make such a stink in front of all our friends and family. My son isn't without faults. He's stubborn as hell sometimes. It's partially my fault he's the way he is." Lila fidgeted with her pearl earring, the smile she'd walked in with long gone.

"When his father left us I shielded Reed from the divorce. Made sure I never cried in front of him. But then he never cried in front of me, trying to act as brave as I was pretending no doubt. We shouldn't have acted, we should have been open and honest. It wasn't good keeping things bottled up inside. I would reassure him that everything would be all right and that we would be just fine. That we would succeed without his father's help."

Sounded like the pep talk Reed had given Hope.

"He overheard me talking to my sister about how his father was getting away with paying little child support or alimony. The next day Reed came home from school and announced he was working at his Uncle Marco's restaurant. From then on, he became the little man of the house, taking on other odd jobs, giving me his paychecks. He used his money to buy clothes so he didn't have to wear rummage sale stuff of kids at school. As much as he tried not to be like his father, and to take care of us, I'm afraid he's turned out too much like his father. He has a ruthless reputation, works much too hard, and money is a priority for him."

Sympathy tugged at Monica's heart. No wonder Reed never showed a vulnerable side.

"So will you plan the reception?" Thoughts of Bill and her marriage brought a smile back to Lila's face.

Monica would feel like she was deceiving Reed if she planned the event. She wished she didn't even *know* about it.

"It's really short notice. I have a lot going on next weekend. I don't know if I'd be able to find a venue." Lila gave her a skeptical look and Monica fessed up. "I don't think I'd feel right planning this when Reed isn't aware that you're married."

Lila gave Monica an approving nod. "You're right. I should tell him before the party. Then would you plan it?"

Monica nibbled at her lower lip.

"Please. I don't know who else I would trust."

Monica nodded. "Don't tell him you came to me first."

Lila smiled. "Agreed."

Acting like she knew nothing about the reception wasn't exactly in line with the open and honest relationship she was striving for with Reed. But it was in line with her desire to hopefully pursue a relationship.

*

A loud thud sounded on the other side of the connecting wall to Reed's office. Startled, Monica jumped in her chair, her gaze darting to the wall. Despite her original fears of yelling and screaming emanating through the wall, this was the first noise she'd heard coming from his office. Reed must have spoken with his mom. Another thud hit the wall and Monica surged from her chair. If Lila was in there, Monica had better go play referee before Reed trashed his entire office.

Monica bolted out past Jordan seated at her desk.

"What the hell was that?" Jordan asked, eying the wall.

"I think Reed just found out his mom got married."

"So much for him being a closet romantic and pro-marriage."

Monica rushed out the door and over to Reed's office. She found him pacing in the middle of his inner office, hands balled into fists at his side, anger radiating from every inch of his body. He was cussing up a storm. A portable phone lay smashed to bits on the floor by their building's common wall. Lila had apparently broken the news over the phone. She probably hadn't cared to see his reaction in person. Monica didn't blame the woman. Seeing

Reed completely out of control was freaking the hell out of her.

"Are you okay?" she asked cautiously, taking a step into his office, wanting to go to him, touch him, comfort him.

He came to an abrupt halt, his gaze darting over to her, his blue eyes darkened with rage. "No, but you already knew that. *Before* I did!"

She flinched. So much for Lila agreeing not to mention she knew about the reception. "It's not my fault she told me she got married."

That was what he was referring to, right? What else would make him go this berserk? And this was the thanks she got for convincing Lila to come clean?

He flexed his fingers, glancing around, as if searching for something else to throw. "I can't believe she'd get married without telling me. And she was pissed at *me* for not telling her I'd had Bill investigated. Pretty damn minor compared to what she did."

"You told her you had Bill investigated?" Monica said in disbelief.

He nodded absently. "She already knew about the divorces. Said she didn't want to tell me because I'd make a big deal out of it. Like being divorced four times isn't a helluva big deal!"

She had to agree there. Not a great track record.

"She bought into all his excuses for the divorces. None of which were his fault of course."

"Maybe he was being honest with her."

He shot her a traitorous look.

"Are you more upset she didn't do a prenup or that she didn't tell you she was getting married?"

A hint of uncertainly flashed across his face, but without missing a beat he said, "Wait 'til I get my hands on that guy."

"It's better that he was divorced four times rather than being widowed four times. Then you'd really have to worry," she tried to lighten the mood.

He looked like that gave him zero comfort.

"Can't you at least get to know Bill, for your mom's sake? She seems to truly love him. Isn't that what really matters?"

He came to an abrupt halt. "Hell no!"

"You don't mean that."

"Yes, I do," he said with his usual confidence.

Okay, his callous attitude was ticking her off. "You're the best damn divorce lawyer in the city and prenup or not you'll protect your mom. You've made what should have been a happy occasion for your mom a totally miserable one."

"As if that's *my* fault."

"Yes, it is. I bet she's at home crying right now when she should be planning her reception. And *that's* not your fault?"

His glare wavered slightly.

"I think maybe you're jealous of Bill. That someone other than you will take care of her for the first time in twenty years."

His jaw tightened. "Jealous? That's bullshit. You don't have a clue."

If she didn't, it was because Reed wouldn't let her in. He had his emotions so well hidden even *he* didn't know how he felt. How the hell was she supposed to know?

"You need to start worrying more about your mom's *emotional* well-being than you do her *financial* well-being. Stop treating her like a client and start treating her like your mom!"

She turned and stormed out of the office.

*

Monica's comment was like a sucker punch to the gut. As if he didn't give a crap about his mother's emotional well-being. Of course he wanted her to be happy. His mother was the only woman he'd ever loved. He'd gone to work at the age of ten to help take care of her. He'd put himself through college to give them both a better life. He'd bought her a house, or at least tried to. He'd built her a nest egg so she'd never have to worry about money . . .

Shit. Was Monica right?

He'd always been there for his mother financially, but what

about emotionally? He raked a frustrated hand through his hair, dropping down in the chair.

It's not like he wasn't involved in his mother's life. He knew her floral arrangement had taken first place in her garden club's summer exhibition. She played bridge every Wednesday. She and her best friend did lunch on Tuesdays. However, he'd never asked her much about Bill. Hell, he wasn't even sure how they'd met. What was it that attracted her to him? What did they do for fun? The only interest he'd shown in Bill was about his divorces.

Could he be jealous of Bill's relationship with his mother? Of the thought that after twenty-one years she could come to rely on Bill more than him?

His mother claimed Bill had honored her wish not to tell Reed about the wedding even though he hadn't agreed with her. He wasn't sure if that was the truth or his mother's attempt at redeeming Bill in his eyes. He wasn't prepared to accept Bill; however, he could accept the fact he'd been a real ass to his mother. The thought of his mother at home crying because of him wrenched his gut. He removed the BlackBerry from the holder at his waist and hit the speed dial.

Chapter Seventeen

Reed stepped out of the French doors and onto the back terrace of his large stone house—or rather mansion. Monica's breath caught in her throat. Wow. Humphrey Bogart incarnate. With his black tux and bowtie, and his dark hair slicked back, he looked even yummier than Bogart had at the Larrabees' garden party in *Sabrina*.

His look was a definite sign they were in tune, at least when it came to their costumes. But was he still ticked?

Monica swept a nervous hand down her strapless, white satin column gown and rested it on the flowing detachable train made of silk organdy. The bodice, skirt, and train were embroidered with a floral design of black silk thread and jet beads. A replica of the dress Audrey Hepburn had worn to the Larrabees' party. The dress that had caused Linus to begin falling madly in love with Sabrina. Hopefully it worked the same magic on Reed, placing him under Monica's spell. Her *soul mate* spell.

Had the spell brought Reed into her life?

Oh man, she hoped so. She couldn't avoid her feelings for him, and no way could Reed avoid her in this dress. Not the most practical dress for her to be running around working a reception in, but when Lila had requested guests dress like their favorite classic romance movie character Monica had immediately surfed the web and found a rental company with this dress. Hopefully the dress did the job.

She'd barely seen Reed over the past week and a half. Not since their conversation when she'd pretty much told him he was a heartless, emotionless bastard. Her comments had apparently hit home because an hour later Lila had phoned and told her the reception was being held at Reed's home. Monica hadn't been avoiding him, she'd been busy planning the reception, along with all her other events. However, Reed had likely been avoiding her. Whenever she'd stopped by his house while planning the reception, even during the evenings, he was nowhere around. He'd given his mom carte blanche use of his lawn and credit card, preferring not to be bothered with the planning, or Monica it seemed.

Reed peered across the sprawling lawn and their gazes met. Even at a distance, she could see his jaw drop slightly as his gaze strolled down the length of her dress then back up, leaving a wake of heat sizzling across her skin.

He was definitely acknowledging her.

Appearing entranced, he stepped down the stairs. The band, conducting a sound check under the large white tent behind her, began playing Glenn Miller's "Moonlight Serenade." The smooth, lilting sound of the clarinet matched the charismatic manner in which Reed strode toward her. His gaze strayed from hers to once again travel down her dress and back up, an appreciative smile curling the corners of his mouth.

She placed a nervous, long white-gloved hand against her stomach then swept it up over the beaded bodice, following the fluttering rising to her chest and flirting with the bottom of her throat. It felt like a hummingbird hovered inside her, trying to escape.

Reed stopped feet in front of her, giving her an accessing gaze. "You, ah, look . . . " he stuttered in a low, husky voice, "incredible." He raised his gaze to hers.

"Thanks. So do you." She brushed a finger over the hollow of her neck, her pinky skimming along the top of her dress. He glanced down at her bodice and she inhaled deeply, causing her breasts to swell. She slowly exhaled, letting out a faint, contented sigh.

"You were right. I wasn't being the best son."

She nodded faintly, surprised by his admission, unsure how to respond.

"Not sure how I feel about Bill yet, but me hurting my mother because I'm afraid Bill *might* hurt her doesn't make any sense. I was pretty much being a selfish ass."

She continued nodding.

The corners of his mouth curled slightly. "Thanks."

Reed admitting he was wrong and exposing a vulnerable side, possibly for the first time since he was ten years old, caused her heart to do a happy dance. She suppressed an ecstatic grin.

She finally managed to mutter, "Any time." No biggie.

Yeah, right. This was huge!

Appearing a tad nervous, he slid his gaze toward the tent where the catering staff scurried around, putting on the finishing touches. "You did a great job with the decor," he said, changing the subject. "Sounds like a good band."

"Thanks. Hope was a huge help. And your lawn's a beautiful setting."

The focal point, a large stone fountain surrounded by colorful flowerbeds, gurgled happily for the occasion. White twinkle lights wrapped around the trunks of several mature oaks and wove through their branches. Blankets of lights covered the immaculately groomed shrubs around the perimeter of the yard. And lights mingled with ivy trailed over a wooden trellis, the gateway for a path leading to the bluff overlooking Lake Michigan. Not yet dusk, however, the yard was lit up, ready to greet guests.

A few stray strands of hair had loosened from her upswept do and she brushed them behind her ear, her fingers lingering on her neck, catching Reed's gaze. He watched her fingers skim down her neck to rest on her collarbone.

A car door slammed shut, followed by Hope yelling out, "Can you help me with this cake?"

Transported from the Larrabees' garden party back to reality, she and Reed exchanged disappointed glances then forced their gazes from each other and over to Hope lifting the back hatch of her SUV. She had on a long, red velvet gown with a low sequined bust line and feathery poofy sleeves. Same as the one Rhett had forced Scarlett to wear to Ashley's birthday party in *Gone With the Wind*, to showcase the improper woman that she was. A drastic change from Hope's usual floral sundresses and more risqué than Monica's hot pink spandex dress.

Hope was definitely morphing from a meek Melanie into a brazen Scarlett.

"We better help her," Monica said.

They headed across the lawn in silence, the spray of organdy flowing from her waist, rustling as she walked. Luckily, it hadn't rained for two days so her heels weren't sinking into the yard.

A blue sedan pulled in the driveway behind Hope, and Bill and Lila got out of the car. Bill had on a dark suit, tan trench coat, and a black fedora. Lila wore a dark 1940s style suit with a dark wide brimmed hat. Almost identical to the outfits worn by Bogie and Ingrid Bergman in the final scene of *Casablanca* when Rick made Ilsa get on the plane and leave him. Not exactly a happy ending, unlike the ending Lila and Bill hoped for. Monica had suggested Bill wear a black tux and Lila a long white dress with a sheer cropped jacket, like the outfits the actors had worn while dancing in Paris, during their liaison and much happier times. Not to mention, the outfits would be more appropriate for the eighty-some degree weather. But the two had insisted the costumes they'd chosen were much more identifiable with the movie.

When they reached Hope's SUV, Lila and Bill were standing at the back admiring the three-tier carrot cake with a topper of Bogie and Ingrid Bergman dressed identical to Lila and Bill.

"Oh, it's perfect," Lila said, her eyes tearing up.

"Sure is." Bill slipped his arm around Lila's shoulder, giving it an affectionate squeeze.

Reed watched their display of affection, his expression softening, a look of approval on his face. "How about you and I take the cake over to the tent?" he asked Bill.

A stunned expression flashed across Bill's face, but he quickly recovered with a smile. "Sounds like a plan."

Lila smiled appreciatively at Reed. A small gesture, yet a major step for Reed in accepting Bill.

Lila glanced between Reed and Monica. "Don't you two look just perfect." Her eyes teared up again, and she widened them, fanning a hand in front of her face, attempting to dry her eyes.

"I'll show you the tent," Monica told Lila.

"Splendid idea." Lila slipped an arm through Monica's and they headed toward the tent, passing by a tree lit up with twinkle lights. "This is all simply lovely. Thank you again for planning everything." Lila gave Monica's hand a loving pat and leaned over and kissed her on the cheek. "The only thing that could make this more perfect would be if this was Reed's wedding reception." She winked at Monica, giving her hand a squeeze. "Don't give up on him. He'll come around. I can tell he cares a lot about you."

Monica had been hoping she and Reed could go on an actual date together, and here Lila had them getting married? Although Monica had to admit she'd had crazy thoughts of marriage, like when Reed did the mock proposal on the boat and pretty much every time she was in the same room with him.

Monica smiled, unsure how to respond. She adored this woman, who was openly affectionate and didn't hide her emotions, unlike her son.

When they stepped inside the tent, Lila could no longer hold back and a tear slipped down her cheek. Her gaze darted from the chairs covered in gold satin fabric with gold bows tied around the backs, to the cream linen tablecloths with gold organza silk overlays. Yellow rose petals and white rose sculpted candles floated in a frosted bowl in the middle of each table.

"It's perfect," Lila said, hand to her chest.

Yes, it was. And the evening would be perfect. If any issues came up, Monica was confident she could troubleshoot them. Her business was going to be a huge success.

Hopefully, her evening with Reed would be also.

*

An hour later, the reception was in full swing. The band was playing "When You Wish Upon a Star" as dusk settled in and twinkle lights danced across the backyard, a backdrop to the dimly lit tent oozing ambiance. Champagne flowed freely down a fountain of glasses and a hundred or so chitchatting guests grazed at a variety of food stations.

Monica had been so busy ensuring the food and bars were set, the waiters were circulating with appetizers and champagne, and everything was running smoothly, that she hadn't had time to talk to Reed. She spied him across the tent talking with an elderly couple, playing the dutiful host, making the rounds. He smiled, and let out a hearty laugh that carried over to her and warmed her inside. He took a sip of champagne, his lower lip pressed against the rim of the glass. She licked her lips, tasting the remnants of the champagne she'd taste tested earlier, certain his lips tasted better. Apparently feeling her gaze on him, he glanced over at her. Rather than being embarrassed and looking away, she held his gaze. He smiled a slow, seductive smile that would have put Rhett Butler to shame.

"I think he's here," Jordan said, materializing at Monica's side.

Monica reluctantly turned her gaze on her friend. "Who?"

"Bogie." Jordan scooped up a spoonful of mashed potatoes topped with mac and cheese, served in a martini glass. She took a bite, savoring it. Monica had been eyeing the merlot mushroom sauce topping earlier, but her stomach was too jittery to eat.

"What are you talking about?"

"I can feel him." With a whoo-whoo, mysterious expression, Jordan glanced around, as if waiting for an apparition to materialize. "I channeled him, inviting him to the party and I'm certain he's here."

Monica did a mental eye roll.

Hope walked up, eyeing Jordan's dress slash costume. It was a flouncing, frilly white lace dress with small silk flowers adorning the low-cut bust line and one big honking one in the middle of it. It looked like something worn by a southern belle or a bridesmaid in the '70s. A wide brimmed straw hat covered the ringlets in her hair.

"So who are you?" Hope asked. "Scarlett O'Hara?"

Jordan shook her head. "Rebecca."

"Oh, yeah, I saw that movie. The scene where that wretched housekeeper cons the new wife into wearing the same costume the dead wife wore right before she died. And then she tries to get her to commit suicide to boot." Hope swirled a marshmallow around in a puddle of melted chocolate on a plate. The chocolate fountain was for sure the biggest hit of the food stations.

"That's me. The dead wife."

Of course it was. Jordan had probably channeled the fictional character also.

"I'll tell ya one couple we for sure don't have to ask who they're supposed to be." Hope shot a discreet glance across the room at a plump couple dressed like Shrek and Fiona, green skin and all. "Aren't they like the cutest couple ever?"

"Guess Lila never specified it had to be an older classic movie," Monica said. "And it was a pretty romantic movie."

Jordan glanced around, taking it all in. "We done good, girls."

"Couldn't have done it without your guys' help," Monica said. "Thanks."

An inspired look consumed Hope's face. "I've thought of what I want to do. A branch of Enhance Your Romance. I could be a wedding planner. You could do the engagement proposals and then I could plan the weddings."

Monica nodded thoughtfully. "Might work."

"I still haven't given up on Bring Your Romance Back to Life." Jordan proceeded to explain her idea to Hope.

Reed walked up on stage and the music faded. His gaze singled out Monica for several moments before he scanned the crowd of guests. "I'd like to thank everyone for coming tonight and joining us in this celebration." He nodded at the piano player behind him and said, "Play it once, Sam. For old times' sake,"

The man knew how to stick with a theme.

"As Time Goes By" played quietly in the background as he began speaking. "Rather than a fog blanketed airport in Casablanca, we're in a bright, airy tent in Milwaukee. Still, the love in the air is as palpable as the last scene of the movie. Lila and Bill didn't meet years ago in Paris, but rather three months ago when she dropped her buns at Pick 'n Save and he picked them up." This elicited a soft chuckle from the guests. "Unlike Ilsa getting on a plane without Rick, Lila and Bill will be getting on a plane together for Paris tomorrow. So, Mom, 'kiss him. Kiss him as if it were the last time, '" he paraphrased Ilsa's line to Rick, glancing between his mom and Bill. "But it won't be the last time. Here's to many more kisses to come. Congratulations." He raised his flute in toast and the guests followed.

Bill and Lila kissed. Monica wiped away the hot tears escaping down her cheeks.

"Holy cow," Jordan muttered, wiping away a tear. "How romantic was that? Maybe I don't need to channel the real Bogie after all."

Hope sniffled, dabbing at her nose with a dainty red-gloved hand. "You two so have to get together. If you don't, I'm going for him."

Monica shot them both a surprised look. She'd never discussed her and Reed with either one of them.

Jordan tapped the side of her head, stating she could see all and Hope said, "I don't need to be psychic to know there's something hot and heavy going on between you two."

"I really don't need to be either," Jordan said. "You haven't sprinkled patchouli oil on the lilac bush in days and all he has to do is walk by the office and you're panting like a puppy in the window." Monica opened her mouth to protest and Jordan cut her off. "Don't deny it."

Monica let out a defeated sigh. "I do not pant."

Reed walked down the stairs of the stage and a woman dressed as Holly Golightly from *Breakfast at Tiffany's* approached him for the dozenth time that night. The chick was certainly persistent. Reed appeared to brush her off, leaving her standing there with a rejected look on her face as he headed Monica's way.

The band played "Moon River" and Lila and Bill began waltzing around the dance floor.

Reed approached and their gazes locked. Monica's body went on red alert, palms sweating, mouth dry. He stopped in front of her, extending a hand toward her. "May I have this dance?"

Her heart sank. "I don't know how to waltz." She knew she should have squeezed in some Arthur Murray dance lessons this past week.

"Neither do I. We'll make good partners."

Partners?

Jordan nudged one of Monica's elbows, Hope the other. Monica placed a white-gloved hand in Reed's, wishing she'd taken off the gloves so she could feel the warmth of his hand wrapped around hers. She slid her other hand up his arm, molding it around his shoulder from the back. He slipped a hand around her waist, maintaining distance between them.

"Better not hold you too close or I might step on your dress," he said.

Suddenly, the dress was working against her plan of seducing Reed. And tripping over the train would certainly kill the mood. Hands clasped out at their sides, held in close proximity to their bodies, they began slowly gliding around the dance floor. Neither had a clue how to waltz yet their steps were in sync, slower than their fellow dancers.

"That was a lovely speech," she said, peering up at him.

He smiled, lines crinkling around his blue eyes. "Thanks. I was a bit nervous."

"It didn't show."

As if he ever looked anything other than cool and confident. Was he nervous now, holding her so closely? Was his stomach fluttering like hers? Did he have the urge to *kiss her. Kiss her as if it were the last time?* The thought of him actually kissing her for the last time gave her a hollow, empty feeling in her chest. She didn't want it to ever be the last time. She wanted more steamy kisses in the rain, on his boat, on her thighs . . . She wanted more kisses everywhere. She adjusted her hand gently against his shoulder, wanting to sweep it up over his neck and skim it across his freshly shaven jaw line. Probably a good thing she had on gloves so he couldn't feel her palms sweating.

She glanced over at his mom and Bill. "They seem really happy. And he seems to truly love her."

Reed nodded. "He better."

"I'm sure your mom and Bill loved their present. Where will they be staying in Paris?"

"A boutique hotel. Upscale yet not pretentious or flashy. *Très romantique.*"

She about melted at the sound of him speaking French.

"What was it the mime had written in the rose?"

She knew damn well what it had said, since the words had been running through her head non-stop, French accent and all, like some foreign flick. Sometimes they were accompanied by visions of her and Reed kissing passionately while strolling along the Seine in Paris, or at a cozy sidewalk café while enjoying a bottle of outrageously expensive champagne. Regardless of their locale, he always spoke the words in a soft, breathless, can't-live-without-you tone against her ear.

She wanted to hear him say the words again, over and over and over . . .

He gazed deep into her eyes, caressing his thumb against the back of her hand. "*Je t'aime,*" he said softly with a French lilt to his voice.

I love you sounded even ten times more passionate when

spoken in French. Yet, he could murder the words in Japanese for all she cared, she suddenly realized she just wanted him to say them and mean them.

"Oh, yeah, *je t'aime*." I love you.

She licked her lips as if she could taste the sweetness of the words playing on her lips and over in her head, with the romantic, lilting sound of "Moon River" in the background. They floated around the dance floor, their bodies in tune, like they'd danced together for fifty years. He swept his hand up her back and down to her waist. She envisioned them dancing alone on the back terrace of his home, spotlighted by the full moon.

They suddenly realized "Moon River" had ended and Glenn Miller's lively "In the Mood" was playing. They slowly came to a stop in the middle of the dance floor, both of them apparently noticing their fellow dancers for the first time. They released their hands, lowering them to their sides. Reed's other arm remained wrapped around her waist and he drew her closer, now that they weren't dancing and had no worries of her dress getting in the way. He gazed deep into her eyes.

Omigod. Was he going to kiss her right there on the dance floor? In front of everyone?

"Thanks for the dance," he said in a low, sexy voice.

She merely nodded.

After several moments of silence, she cleared her throat. "I should probably go check on the caterer. See if the coffee is coming out so we can cut the cake."

After all, she was working.

He slowly slipped his hand from around her waist and stepped back. "Cake looks good." He eyed her with a hunger, as if maybe she looked tastier than the cake.

He certainly did.

Chapter Eighteen

Reed stepped out the French doors and onto the terrace. He peered over at the brightly lit tent where the décor company was loading tables and chairs into the truck backed up on the lawn. Monica wasn't in the kitchen or the tent. Had she decided not to stick around for the tear down and left without saying goodbye? No way had he misread the signals she'd been sending him all night. They were loud and clear. She wanted him as badly as he wanted her.

Maybe deep down she was pissed and confused that he'd avoided her over the past week because he feared she was making him a wuss. Not seeing Monica certainly hadn't made him feel more *manly*. Unlike being with her, which made him damn happy he was a man. He hadn't realized how much he'd missed her until he'd laid eyes on her tonight. And it wasn't just the ambiance and how friggin' incredible she looked in that dress. She could have on a wrinkled white cotton shirt and pink capris, and major helmet hair, like the day they'd met, and she'd still turn him on. She was sexy as hell, but even more so he was attracted to her spunk, determination, and her ability to straighten him out when he was being an ass.

Something a woman had never before succeeded at doing.

He glanced around the yard, toward the bluff overlooking Lake Michigan. There she stood, her slender form silhouetted by the full moon. The train no longer attached to her dress, he could see the curves of her body even from the distance. A breeze carried the moonlight rippling across the lake and an intense desire surged through him.

He had to have her.

He walked down the steps and headed across the lawn toward the bluff. Monica's pull on him was stronger than the moon's gravitational pull on the earth. With each step, he felt his self-control diminish while his need for her grew stronger.

As he approached she turned around, startled, hand to her chest. Precisely where he wanted his hand to be. "Sorry," he said softly. "Didn't mean to sneak up on you."

She smiled, shaking her head, as if to say *no problem.* She turned back to the lake. "Awesome view." A breeze blew off the lake and she folded her arms across her front, shivering slightly.

He slipped off his tux jacket. Standing behind her, he held it out for her. She peered over her shoulder at the jacket then up at him beneath her thick lashes. She slipped her arms in the sleeves and he slid the jacket on her.

"Thanks," she muttered.

"Sure."

His arms still encompassing her, his hands curled around the jacket's lapels, resting against her collarbone, just above the top of her bodice. He slid his hands up and down the lapels, his fingers grazing her skin. Her breath hitched in her throat, her chest expanding against his hands. She slowly exhaled air along with a contented moan, urging him on.

He placed a gentle kiss against the side of her neck and she rolled her head to the side, fully exposing her neck. The exotic, spicy scent of her perfume lured him up her neck and he nuzzled behind her ear. He traced the tip of his tongue along the contour of her ear and she let out another moan, covering his hands with hers, pressing them firmly against her breasts.

Wisps of her hair teased his cheek, flirting with it. He trailed kisses to the front of her neck as he slowly circled around, facing her, slipping his hands beneath the suit jacket to the curves of her waist. Her soft body molded against him. She slid her hands up his arms and around the back of his shoulders, cupping them from behind, her fingers kneading the muscles.

Her head tilted back in submission and he continued kisses up her neck, over her chin to her mouth. He licked her soft, moist lips before slipping his tongue inside the warmth of her mouth and stroking her tongue. She tasted like champagne and his wildest erotic dreams. She deepened the kiss, wrapping her tongue around his. Drawing his head back slightly, he opened his eyes to find the moonlight casting a blue glow against her pale smooth skin. She looked almost mystical. Appropriate, since he couldn't believe what was happening between them was for real. He'd never dreamed he'd ever feel this way about a woman.

He placed a kiss to her eyelids, then down over her sculpted cheekbones, to the dip above her upper lip. Her eyelids fluttered open and moonlight reflected in her soft brown eyes. God, she was gorgeous. He'd take her right there if it weren't for the décor company in the tent. He glanced over to find the tent dark, the truck gone. Moonlight lit the yard, however, a natural fence of trees and shrubs provided privacy from neighbors. Yet, he wanted her in his bed, where he'd never had a woman before.

He slipped his hands from her waist preparing to take hold of her hand, but she reached her hands behind her back and slowly unzipped her dress. She grasped the material at her hips and gave the dress a solid tug then shimmied it off, letting it puddle on the ground. She stepped from the dress, standing there in killer black heels, a white lace strapless bra and thong, and his black tux jacket. Moonlight washed over her nearly naked body.

They'd make love in his bed next.

"Jacket looks much better on you," he said.

"Would look even better off."

"Without a doubt."

*

Reed slipped his hands under the jacket and skimmed them up over her breasts to her shoulders, sliding them down her arms, taking the jacket with them. He dropped it and she stood there in her undies and heels. His heated gaze warmed the faint breeze that blew up from the lake. An arctic blast couldn't cool her down right now. If her skin were anymore on fire, it'd be singeing the hairs on her arms.

Silhouetted by the moonlight behind him, he looked sexier and more charismatic than any leading man in a classic romance movie. He appeared larger than life. Like he'd just heroically scaled the side of the bluff, coming to her rescue.

He *had* rescued her.

Rescued her from believing she'd never find someone who could make her insides melt with a mere glance. Rescued her from the deep seated fear she'd never fall in love . . .

Omigod. She *loved* Reed.

She loved the way his lips felt against hers. His gentle, attentive touch. His unwavering confidence in her ability to succeed. His cologne, his ties . . .

She just plain loved him.

His gaze narrowed in concern from the undoubtedly freaked out expression on her face. "Something wrong?"

If loving him was wrong, then yes, she had one helluva problem on her hands. But it didn't feel wrong. It felt insanely right. She shook her head.

A sexy smile curled the corners of his mouth as he freed her hair from the clip and it tumbled to her shoulders. He tunneled his fingers through her hair before cupping the sides of her head.

"Kiss me," she said in a breathless, steamy voice. "Kiss me as if it were the last time."

"This is far from the last time."

His mouth seized hers with a greedy hunger and he undid her strapless bra and it dropped to the ground. She yanked off his bowtie and sent it flying, likely over the side of the cliff. While she frantically undid his oxford buttons, his hands were all over her. She had his shirt off and was onto his pants in seconds flat. Clothes were flying like they were lovers reunited after *years* of separation rather than a week and a half. Not merely seeking to physically, but also emotionally, reconnect. This wasn't about lust.

She undid his pants and his hands strayed just long enough to strip them off, along with his boxers. Monica went to kick off her heels.

"Keep 'em on," Reed said, his gaze traveling down over her naked body to her feet.

One of his sexual fantasies no doubt.

Their nearly naked bodies molded together, they lowered themselves to the ground. On her back, the dry grass prickled her skin, but she'd lie on a bed of broken glass to be with Reed. He slipped his hands under her knees, drawing her legs up as he trailed kisses along her inner thigh to the front of her thong, already moist with anticipation.

He reached over and snagged a condom from the back pocket of his pants. Bracing his forearms on either side of her, he lowered his body, easing himself inside her. Her breath caught in her throat, bringing a pleased smile to his face. Holding her gaze, he eased out then slowly back in, gently thrusting deeper each time until he was filling her completely. He wrapped his leg around hers as he rolled onto his back taking her with him, still inside her. Now on top, but feeling even less in control, she drew her knees up alongside him, straddling him. He placed his hands on her hips guiding her, raising his hips to meet her with each thrust.

His thrusts became more powerful, his grip on her hips firmer. Her back arched and the rhythm of their bodies increased. Her head dropped back and her eyes glazed over. He let out several deep-throated moans and his body tensed then shuddered beneath hers, his hands still gripping her hips. Moments later, a shockwave of trembles convulsed her body, and she wilted against his body, pressing her soft breasts against his chest. She nuzzled her head next to his.

"Un-believable," she muttered against his ear.

"Oh yeah." He placed a hot kiss to her temple. "You're beyond unbelievable."

No. The two of them *together* was beyond unbelievable.

So was the fact she loved Reed.

Chapter Nineteen

Reed blinked the sleep from his eyes, squinting back the daylight pouring through the open drapes into his bedroom. The glaring sunlight was a rude awakening, unlike the exotic, spicy traces of Monica's scent on his pillow, evoking memories of the hottest sex ever. He rolled onto his side, toward the pillow beside him, preparing to initiate another marathon round of lovemaking. Rather than Monica's chestnut hair spread out on the pillow, and her naked body wrapped in the cotton sheets, there was merely a slight indentation on the bed where she'd laid.

Monica was gone.

He bolted upright, his gaze darting over to the floor, verifying that only *his* clothes remained strewn across the carpet. A sick feeling wrenched his gut. So this was what it felt like to be the one left alone in bed after sex. He didn't like it one damn bit. Not because it bruised his ego that a *woman* could be the one to leave *him* hungry for more. He'd wanted to wake up next to Monica. To be inside her again. To talk. To discuss what was happening between the two of them and where they were going. Their future.

After last night, they definitely had a future.

So why had she left? Why did *he* always leave a woman before she woke up? Hell, he usually left before she went to sleep. He left because he didn't want women to have any expectations of him, like delusional thoughts of commitment. He'd never met a woman he'd wanted to be committed to, until now. That certainly wasn't Monica's issue. She was all about commitment, forever, till death do us part. But she also knew that had always been the furthest thing from his mind. Maybe she thought he would wake up with regrets.

He'd thought he might himself until just now.

Maybe he shouldn't have freaked out over finding himself more in tune with his clients. Maybe this could somehow make him a stronger, not a weaker lawyer. Right now, if it came down to losing his edge or losing Monica, he was fairly certain he'd choose to lose his edge.

He grabbed the phone off the nightstand, glancing at the clock. 5:42 A.M. They'd only gone to sleep three hours ago. Or at least he had. Had she left before even falling asleep? He didn't know her home number or her cell. He dialed 4-1-1, praying like hell her number was listed. He had to talk to her.

*

Monica peered out the leaded glass window of Reed's front door, as if watching for a taxi to pull into the driveway at any moment. Not likely, since she hadn't called one. She'd been standing there a half hour, torn between making an exit or going back upstairs and slipping into bed with Reed, nestling her head against his broad chest, wrapping her leg around his, snuggling against the warmth of his body. She slid her gaze over her shoulder and up the sweeping staircase, covered with red oriental carpeting. You'd think the decision would be a no-brainer.

Go back upstairs!

However, she wanted to remember last night as the most magical night ever. She didn't want reality to set in. She didn't want Reed to wake up and announce he had a divorce court hearing to get to and then she'd agree that yes, she had to get going because she had eleven engagement proposals to plan. She wanted to avoid reality as long as possible. One of the reasons last night was so incredible was because they'd barely spoken. No shop talk or discussion of their differences. She feared talking would ruin the physical and emotional connection they'd shared, so she'd left. The bedroom anyway.

Still peering up the stairs, she imagined Reed's lips touching hers, then softly kissing her breasts, lower to her abdomen, her . . . She gave herself a mental fanning, her cheeks and neck on fire. Her gaze shot up to the ceiling, in the direction of Reed's bedroom.

She took a mint from her purse and popped it in her mouth, then swept a comb through her bed head of hair. She looked like total crap. Did she really want him to see her like this?

Her gaze strolled back down the stairs, sweeping over the Gauguin and Picasso reproductions lining the red wall, and the large potted fern at the bottom. His house was cozy and not at all as modern and sterile as she'd expected.

She glanced back out at the driveway.

What if this was only a fling for him? That scared her more than anything. Standing here by the door for the past half hour reconfirmed she sucked at flings. She needed to leave before he woke up, relieved she was gone. Leave with her head held high, her self-respect and heart still somewhat intact.

Leave before she told Reed she loved him and he gave her a panicked look, unable to reciprocate her feelings.

"Isn't It Romantic" blared out from her black clutch, shattering the peaceful morning air, echoing off the walls up to the expansive ceiling. She'd turned her cell phone up loud last night so she could hear it over the band. She scrambled to answer the phone before it woke up Reed. It was likely Hope wondering where she was. The laundry fairy had probably crept into Monica's room to empty the hampers and noticed she'd never come home. Monica snatched the phone from her purse as it stopped ringing and displayed one missed call. She checked the number, not recognizing it. While she scrolled through her mental phone book, it rang again. She answered it.

"Come back to bed," Reed said, his voice low and raspy from sleep, sounding even sexier than usual. The invitation caused her inner thighs to throb and her heart to race at the fact he hadn't been relieved to wake up and find her gone. She'd given him an out and he hadn't taken it.

He'd obviously heard her cell phone go off. She could lie and say her taxi was there and escape out the door. However, she had to face him either here or at the office. And the prospect of crawling back in bed with him definitely had her leaning toward here. Although the office would provide a more neutral ground for a realistic discussion about their future, not merely their physical attraction.

"I, ah, have to get to work." Her voice was breathless and far from convincing.

"If you go to work, I can't make love to you again."

Her breath hitched in her throat and she skimmed her hand down over her neck to her breasts, resting it there, letting out a contented moan.

"Why don't you let me do that?" Reed's voice, oozing sex appeal, came from the top of the stairs, rather than the other end of the line.

She slowly lowered the phone from her ear, and her hand from her breast, turning toward the staircase. She raised her gaze to the top of the stairs where Reed stood peering down at her. He wore a lazy, seductive smile and a pair of black silk pajama bottoms resting low on his waist, no top.

She snapped her phone shut.

Her gaze focused on the pajama's string resting against the front of the silk bottoms. Her gaze slid up, caressing the muscles in his abs and chest before continuing up to his mouth and finally meeting his blue eyes filled with a lustful hunger.

"Can't believe you were going to leave without saying goodbye." Wearing a slightly wounded expression, he started down the stairs toward her, his gaze never drifting from hers.

"I, ah, didn't want to wake you. We didn't get much . . . sleep." Bringing up the hot sex they'd been going at till three in the morning wasn't exactly the way to keep the focus off of their physical relationship.

He quirked a suggestive brow. "We certainly didn't." He hit the bottom of the stairs and continued toward her, stopping inches in front of her, the scent of jasmine cocooning her body. "And since we're wide awake now . . . " He reached out and grazed the back of his fingers over her cheek and she let out a barely audible sigh.

"I . . . really should get going." Her gaze probably had more steam coming off it than a pot of boiling water. Not real convincing.

He tilted his head to the side, studying her, as if reading her thoughts. "We'll make this work." As usual, his voice exuded complete confidence. He cupped the side of her face in his palm, massaging a thumb over her lips. She slid the tip of her tongue across the pad of this thumb.

She somehow managed to reign in her excitement and not throw herself in his arms. "We will?"

He nodded, a reassuring smile curling the corners of his mouth. "Yeah, we will."

He skimmed his hands down over the curves of her breasts to the sides of her waist, then slipped them around to rest on the small of her back. He pulled her snuggly against him. She fanned her hands across his chest, splaying her fingers through the vee of dark hair, flexing her fingertips against his chest.

"I'll move my office," he said. "Distance makes the heart grow fonder."

"I don't want you to move." She'd been trying to get him to move since day one and now she was begging him to stay?

He wore a surprised, yet pleased expression. "Really?"

She nodded.

"I think it might help." He leaned over and kissed her gently.

"Let's discuss it later," she murmured against his lips.

Their kiss deepened and he eased the zipper down the back of her dress. Oh yeah, she so didn't feel like talking right now . . .

Chapter Twenty

Monica was way late for work. She hadn't left Reed's until almost eight o'clock and upon arriving home, Hope had grilled her, wondering if Reed was as awesome in bed as he looked like he'd be. Since he'd called looking for Monica's cell phone number at five thirty in the morning, Monica really couldn't deny where she'd spent the night. Still giddy, Monica gave Hope the abbreviated version, wanting to keep the intimate details between her and Reed, but confirming that oh yeah, Reed was even better in bed than he advertised.

Now almost nine o'clock, Monica parked her scooter down the street from her office. She slipped off her helmet and stuck it beneath the seat. She foofed her hair, tilting her face toward the sunshine, inhaling the scent of freshly mown grass and breakfast burritos wafting out of Chico's restaurant. She was in such a great mood she expected a cartoon bluebird to land on her shoulder and for them to break into song and dance.

Dance . . . waltz . . . moonlight . . . steamy kisses . . . making love . . .

Every thought she had somehow reminded her of last night. Or this morning, when Reed had assured her their relationship would succeed. His usual confidence had erased any doubts. They would make this work regardless of their differences. Her entire body went warm all over. Without a doubt, she loved him. He must love her. She'd felt it in the way he'd looked at her like she was the only woman in the tent while they'd danced. In the way he'd touched her while making love. And she'd heard it in his voice when he'd asked her to come back to bed that morning. She'd been prepared to leave, giving him the opportunity to walk away, or rather let her walk away, and he hadn't. However, he'd cared enough to offer to move away.

With a wide grin on her face, she strolled up the sidewalk toward her office. A woman in a tan suit holding a tape recorder, and a guy with a high-tech camera snapping photos, bolted across the street.

"Excuse me, Ms. Bartolli?" the woman called out.

A pretty blonde in a white form-fitting dress stopped on the sidewalk between Monica and Reed's offices.

The woman, a reporter it appeared, thrust the recorder in the other woman's face. "Is it true you filed for divorce from your husband Vincent Bartolli, the owner of Bartolli Construction?"

Curious as to what type of woman was married to such a complete ass, and wanting to hear her rip him to shreds, Monica slipped inside the entryway to her building, spying on them.

The blonde squared her narrow shoulders, raised her sculpted chin, and pursed her full lips. "Yes, it is." She gave a pert nod for emphasis, but the quiver in her voice gave away the confident demeanor she was striving for.

"Your husband was listed as one of the wealthiest men in Wisconsin last year. Do you think he'll be sharing that wealth with you?"

Nibbling at her lower lip, Ms. Bartolli rubbed a nervous hand over her throat, displaying the two-carat diamond wedding ring devouring her dainty finger. Interesting, she still had on her ring. "Vinnie is a very generous man." Her voice was filled with compassion and adoration for her husband. "He always buys—" She snapped her mouth shut and swallowed hard before continuing. "*Bought* me gifts."

"Having one of the best divorce lawyers in the city should help. Your husband has no problem with his own son representing you?"

Son?! Reed was Vincent Bartolli's *son*? Reed Bartolli? She so did not like the sound of that. Why hadn't Reed mentioned this the day she'd confronted him about representing Vincent Bartolli? Because they'd barely known each other, but now things were different. He'd had plenty of opportunities to confide in her about his dad. And his mom feared he'd turned out just like this man?

Monica refused to believe that. Vincent Bartolli was a ruthless bastard, willing to screw over anybody to get what he wanted. Yet she had to admit, Reed was a tad ruthless. Look at his license plate, the sign in his window, and his cutthroat reputation. And he was definitely a workaholic and money hungry.

However, he was also compassionate and *very* passionate. He'd had Monica console a potential client. Maybe that had been because he couldn't get her out of his office and not because he'd been concerned about her welfare. But he'd also helped Monica with Chad's romantic engagement proposal. His toast at his mother's reception had been the most romantic ever. And he'd offered to move for her.

"He's fine with Reed representing me in our," a pained look narrowed her perfectly sculpted brows, "divorce." Her nose wrinkled as if the word divorce caused an icky taste in her mouth.

Omigod. She was still in love with the prick.

Reed bolted out of his office, thrusting a protective arm in front of his client. "What the hell's going on here?"

The reporter didn't miss a beat, turning her recorder toward him. "Mr. Walker, could you tell me—"

"I won't be telling you a damn thing, nor will Ms. Bartolli." Reed's look sharpened, warning the reporter to back off. He directed his client to escape into his office and she scurried inside, her pink Jimmy Choos clicking frantically against the cement sidewalk.

Monica inched further back into the alcove, not wanting Reed to spot her.

"So," the reporter said, "this must cause a bit of a family rift for you to be representing your stepmom rather than your father. Your father has Sandusky and Reinholdt, the largest and most prominent firm in the city representing him. Doesn't that worry you?"

Reed stopped shy of entering his office and spun back around, stabbing a finger at her. "I handled eighty-two divorces last year, many of which Sandusky and Reinholdt were opposing council on. Landed one client a twenty-two million dollar settlement and another ten mil. Do I sound like a man who's worried?" He gestured to the reporter's ring. "How long you been married?"

She looked taken back by the question. "Ah, twelve years."

He removed a gold business card holder from his jacket pocket, slipped out a card, and handed it to her. "You only have a fifty-two percent chance of making it to fifteen years. I'm sure I'll be hearing from you soon."

Monica's stomach tossed and she slapped a hand over her mouth, afraid she was gonna be ill. He sounded like the cynical, down-on-love lawyer she'd first met, spewing negative statistics. Not the same man who'd wrapped her in the warmth of his arms that morning and promised they would make things work. If he believed divorce was so inevitable, how did he figure their relationship would work out?

Very poorly obviously.

Stunned, mouth gaping, the reporter dropped her hand with the recorder to her side. She turned to the photographer. "Come on. We're outta here." They stalked off across the street.

Monica, on the other hand, had plenty she wanted to say to Reed. She stepped out from the alcove. "So hypothetically, if we got married, what would our chance be of making it even five years? Statistically."

Reed's gaze darted over to her, surprise and concern replacing the angry scowl contorting his features. "How long you been standing there?"

"What, maybe a seventy-five percent chance?"

He let out a defeated sigh, looking like he was screwed no matter what he said. "Eighty-two percent. So only an eighteen percent chance we *wouldn't* make it."

"How about ten years?"

"Sixty-five percent." He took a step toward her. The scent of jasmine caressed her body like Reed had that morning on the entryway floor and against the wall, like a couple of wild animals. "We'll make it." The flicker of doubt in his eyes betrayed his confident tone.

How could they succeed when he had more faith in statistics than relationships? She wasn't naïve enough to expect a fairytale romance. All relationships had problems, nothing was a guarantee, but she'd like to think she had better than a fifty percent shot at a happy ending. Their relationship could never end in marriage unless Reed believed his marriage wouldn't end in divorce. And *that* would never happen.

She stepped back, unable to think clearly with him so close. She needed to think, not *feel* right now. And when she was near Reed feelings of love, passion, and lust overshadowed all rational reasoning.

"Why didn't you tell me Vincent Bartolli's your father?" She tried hard to sound ticked off rather than hurt he hadn't confided in her.

He dropped his head back, letting out a frustrated groan, like he couldn't believe they were having this conversation. He gazed around. "Not something I'm really proud of."

Understandable, but still.

She nibbled at her lower lip, debating her next move. She didn't want a major confrontation. The thought of never feeling his touch again caused a sick, hollow feeling in her body, like her organs were shutting down. As if she literally needed Reed to survive. But she felt an ethical obligation to ask a question, and she needed to hear his response.

"I don't think his wife is certain about this divorce."

"Believe me, she's certain," he said with the same air of confidence he'd guaranteed her that morning that their relationship would succeed.

"Have you actually asked her?"

"Yes, I have." He glanced down the street, avoiding her gaze. His gaze darted around while he repeatedly clenched his hands into fists and relaxed them. When he appeared to have control of his anger, he peered back over at her. "I offered to move, so not like you need to *save* a third couple." His tone came off condescending, as if her work was trivial.

"I'm not doing this because of the bet, I'm just saying I think she's having doubts and you should talk to her about it. Make sure you don't want the divorce more than she does."

Reed's jaw tightened. "I do not want the divorce more than she does."

"Believe me, I'd like to see her take her husband to the cleaners, but what if she still loves the guy? Why don't we ask her how she feels?" She took a step toward his office and he moved in front of her, pressing a halting hand out in front him.

"Listen." The low, dead serious tone of his voice sent a chill up her spine. "I don't interfere with your clients, so I'd appreciate you not interfering with mine, okay? This is business, don't make it personal."

This was sooo personal. This spoke volumes about Reed and their relationship. This side of him scared the bejeezus out of her. She wanted the Reed back who sang pub songs, made romantic toasts, and made love to her in the moonlight. The corners of her mouth twitched and she fought back the tears threatening the rims of her eyes. "*Have* you turned out like your dad?" she muttered softly, not wanting to believe it.

A wild expression seized his face and gone was any trace of the man she'd made love to mere hours earlier. "I'm *nothing* like that man," he seethed.

"You seem to care more about work and money than your clients. And you're so angry, hell bent on revenge."

"I care about him doing right by his wife and not screwing her over like . . . " he trailed off, leaving the words *he did my mom and I* unsaid, but she knew that's what he was thinking. "Don't worry about saving a third relationship. I'm outta here. My office is done the end of next month."

"What office?"

"This was only temporary until I got my new office."

And here she'd wanted an open and honest relationship with Reed when it seemed he'd been anything but.

"Why didn't you ever tell me this? Why did you bother making the bet?"

"I like a challenge." A look of regret flashed across his face, yet he still turned and marched inside his office.

Was that all she was professionally and personally? A flippin' challenge? She didn't believe that. However, Reed's cynicism and pessimism were deep-rooted in childhood, not just a side effect of his career. How could Monica expect to undo what would likely take years of therapy, if Reed would agree to therapy, which he wouldn't. He didn't open up to himself, he wasn't about to open up to a therapist.

A sharp pain pierced her chest and she gasped, slapping a hand against her chest. A panic attack. The thought of no longer being able to use making love to Reed as a stress reducer caused a stabbing pain so fierce she sucked in some serious air and flinched.

Whoever said you couldn't die of a broken heart was dead wrong.

Chapter Twenty-One

Monica plastered on what she hoped was an enthusiastic and perky smile while she finished presenting her idea to Chad Martin for his engagement proposal. Or rather her and *Reed's* idea. She tried to shove aside thoughts of Reed's mock engagement proposal and their lovemaking afterward. It was all she could do to keep from having a meltdown.

Chad nodded encouragingly, appearing to be into the proposal. She finished and he smiled wide. "Sweet. Callie is gonna love that. Especially the part where will you marry me lights up along the boardwalk. I owe Reed big time for recommending you." He snapped his mouth snapped shut at the realization he'd let the cat out of the bag. At their initial meeting, he'd claimed to have heard about her company from the newspaper article.

Her eyes about bugged out of her head. "Reed Walker referred you here?"

He nodded. "Yeah, shit man, can't believe I just outed him. He asked me not to say anything. Didn't think you'd accept his help. But hell, I'd have come to you anyway if I'd known about your company. This proposal rocks."

"Thanks," she muttered.

"So can it be ready for next Saturday night? Weather permitting?"

She nodded. "I'll keep an eye on the forecast."

Chad handed her a check for several thousand more than what she'd quoted in her proposal. She'd never had a client pay in full, let alone overpay. "This is too much," she said, offering him back the check.

He shook his head, pushing the check toward her. "It's worth it. Callie's gonna love it. Thanks again."

He walked out and Jordan rushed in, smiling anxiously. "He looked psyched about your idea."

Monica nodded.

"So why the gray aura? I'm talking like this huge arc of gray is hovering over your head."

"He told me Reed referred him here."

Jordan placed a hand to her mouth. "How sweet was that? What's the difference if he heard about you through the article or through Reed?" Her gaze narrowed, the wheels obviously turning in her head. "Actually, you know, I wonder if Reed didn't have something to do with that newspaper article also. I mean that reporter woman seemed kind of fishy when she said she'd seen the office while driving by. Always had a weird feeling about her."

Rather than the career spell, had it been Reed who'd helped her business succeed? She had to admit he'd given her confidence in her abilities. He must care about her to have referred both the reporter and Chad to her company. The fact that he'd done both anonymously, not wanting credit, meant even more. Here she'd been trying to get rid of him and he'd been helping her business take off.

Tears flirted with the rims of her eyes. Unfortunately, this didn't change their future together. Same as a spell, faith and belief were the core ingredients a marriage needed to succeed. All the pixie dust and jasmine oil in the world wouldn't give Reed faith that their marriage wouldn't likely end in divorce.

*

Reed marched through the front door of Bartolli Construction's corporate office. The muted gray and black décor drew people's attention to the color photos lining the walls. Photos dedicated to the company's achievements. Like the one of his father and the mayor at a ribbon cutting for the new downtown arena Bartolli Construction had built five years ago.

Reed now had the chance to take away a major chunk of what the bastard had sacrificed his family and personal life for.

Since his father's lawyer was screwing around in forwarding the corporation's tax returns, Reed decided his father merely needed to know exactly why Reed had requested them. If he didn't want to go to prison for tax evasion, he damn well better give Natalie a generous payout and settle outside of court. This was more of a bluff, since he'd figured his mother would probably be pissed if he got his father thrown in prison. Besides, if he owed a lot in back taxes, Natalie would lose a chunk of her settlement.

A petite, perky brunette manning the receptionist desk smiled as he approached. "Can I help you sir?"

Reed looked past her, spying his father's name engraved on a gold plate on the door at the end of the hallway. "I'm here to see Vincent Bartolli," he said, marching past her desk.

"Wait a second, sir." She surged from her chair. "You need to wait," she demanded, chasing him down the hallway. "Is he expecting you?"

"Doubt it."

When Reed reached the end of the hallway, he threw open the office door and stalked inside, the receptionist hot on his heels. His father glanced up from behind a large desk. A look of surprise flashed across his face then gave way to a combination of fear and panic, like he half expected Reed to whip out a gun and blow him away. If anyone was going to prison, it was his father, not him.

The bastard's strong angular features had mellowed with age and his blue eyes dimmed, but they still held that cold, compassionless stare. Tall and fit, he appeared strong on the outside, but he was a weak coward on the inside. He hadn't even had the guts to tell a ten-year-old he was leaving. Reed had come home from school one day and his mother had explained that his father had gone away, but assured Reed he'd still be seeing him. An optimistic assumption. His father had come around once a month for the first few months and "mailed" Reed a present the first Christmas he was gone. Reed had taken the present to the post office himself and mailed it back.

"I'm sorry Mr. Bartolli," the girl said. "I asked him to wait, but he—"

"That's fine. I'll see him."

The receptionist shot Reed a pissed off look before huffing out.

His father gestured toward the black leather wingback chair in front of his desk. "Have a seat."

"I'll stand."

His father pushed his chair back from the desk and stood, preferring to be on the same footing as Reed no doubt. Wasn't gonna happen.

"Can I get you something to drink?"

"This isn't a social visit."

"Didn't figure it was." His father smoothed a hand down over his conservative yellow and blue striped tie. The man had shitty taste in ties. "Don't blame you for taking Natalie's case. I'd do the same thing if I were you. I'd probably have made it my life goal to try to screw me over." He let out an ironic chuckle. "Guess we're a lot alike in that respect."

A sick taste filled Reed's mouth and his top lip curled back in disgust. "We are *nothing* alike. I don't commit federal offenses that could land me in prison for the rest of my life."

His father arched an intrigued brow. Hadn't his lawyer advised him Reed had requested his corporation's taxes? This was a fairly common request, maybe he hadn't thought anything of it. He probably hadn't given Natalie enough credit to figure out what he was doing.

"I know you've been writing off a shitload of personal expenses, claiming them as business expenses. So if you don't want me to subpoena your company tax returns for the past few years, and dissect them, I suggest you give Natalie the money she rightfully has coming."

Rather than looking worried over having the IRS on his ass, along with some burly guy with prison tattoos, his father let out an amused chuckle. "I'm damn proud of the way you turned out." The pleased look on the man's face made Reed wanna puke.

The last thing Reed wanted was this man's approval.

"Well you can't take any credit for that, can you?"

Like hell he couldn't. After his father had left, Reed went to work at his uncle Marco's out of the need for survival. Earning his own money brought him a sense of respect and fueled his desire for more odd jobs to earn more money. To prove to his father they could succeed without his help. Hell, he was the reason Reed had become a divorce lawyer, wanting justice for the underdog. Every time he landed a client a favorable settlement, it was like a drug he couldn't get enough of. He wanted an even more lucrative settlement for his next client. To right all their spouses' wrongs. His hunger for money and success to throw back in his father's face had made him a pit bull divorce lawyer.

Shit. Monica was right. He *was* just like the bastard. A bitter, ruthless, money obsessed, workaholic who put work before friends and family and was committed to his job rather than to the woman who loved him.

And Reed loved Monica.

But like Reed's mother, she deserved better than his father. And right now, that wasn't Reed.

His father nodded approvingly. "I'd use the exact same tactics you are. So what do you want? An extra million? Maybe two, so you can split it with Natalie?"

As if Reed were after money rather than justice. He clenched his fist, wanting to deck the son of a bitch. The anger eating him up inside had made him someone he didn't like.

Even worse, someone Monica now didn't like.

"I don't want your money for *me*. I've done quite well without it."

"That you have." He gave another nod of approval and Reed's jaw clenched even tighter, his teeth ready to crumble. "Natalie knew what she was getting into when we married."

"She knew you had an ex-wife and kid?"

"No, but she knew work would always come first. I admire the woman. Never thought she'd have the balls to file for divorce.

Maybe I misjudged her." Admiration shown in his eyes. His father seemed to still care for Natalie. God only knew why, but maybe Monica was right and Natalie still loved him.

"Do you still love her? If you ever did."

His father nodded slowly. "Yeah, guess I do."

"Then I suggest you tell her that. And I suggest you treat her right. She might hesitate to bring proof of tax evasion to the D.A., but I won't."

If Natalie decided to pursue the divorce, he wouldn't be her lawyer. He didn't want anything to do with his father and that included getting revenge. Time to let go of the past before it destroyed his future.

If it hadn't already done so.

Chapter Twenty-Two

The following morning Monica pulled up outside her office, immediately noticing the obnoxious sign in Reed's window—*Marriage isn't a word, it's a sentence. I'll set you free*—was gone. So was the one over his door, *Reed Walker: Family Law.*

Her heart, breathing, traffic, the entire world skidded to a halt. The realization was surreal.

Reed was gone.

He sure hadn't wasted any time moving out.

She glared at the lilac bush. The good riddance spell had certainly done its job. She wrapped her hands around the base of the bush where the branches fed into the soil. She gave it a solid tug, loosening the root system slightly. Fueled by anger and pure adrenaline, she pulled on the bush with all her strength. It flew from the soil, along with several dozen green obsidian stones, and she fell back on the sidewalk with a hard thud. It felt like she'd broken her tailbone, but that pain paled in comparison to the pain she felt in her heart. Rather than giving in to her desire to break down and bawl, she stood up and whipped the bush on the ground. After swatting the pebbles and dirt off her butt, she snagged the bush and stalked inside, a trail of dirt falling from the roots.

"Planning on repotting that?" Jordan asked as Monica marched past her desk.

"Unless you have a wood chipper."

Jordan shook her head. "Nope, no wood chipper. Sorry."

Monica marched into her office and repotted the bush, cramming it into the medium size garbage can next to her desk. The top of the bush overflowed from the can.

She took the charm bag out of the top desk drawer and tossed it in with the bush without taking a whiff of it. She needed to cleanse her office of the scent of jasmine, even though the career spell may have worked in a roundabout way, bringing Reed into her life. He'd been good for her business, just not her personally. Since the dirtbag spell had also been a success, she hadn't lost her faith in spells, just the soul mate one in particular. And although she still had faith in spells, and now had faith in herself, her faith in love and marriage was iffy at best. At least when it came to herself. And no amount of jasmine oil or lavender incense held the power to restore that faith.

Only one man did.

*

A few hours later, Monica sat at her desk, glaring at the lilac bush in the garbage. The only thing she'd been able to focus on all morning. She needed some serious comfort food. Maybe some cheese enchiladas, guacamole, and a few strawberry margaritas, or *mucho* margaritas, would make her forget about Reed.

Yeah, right. Not even a Xanax followed by a Prozac chaser could perk her up right now.

"As Time Goes By" jangled. What an annoying song. She needed to look into getting it changed.

For the first time ever, she'd closed the blinds on her office windows and shut the door. She'd given Jordan strict orders to keep away all optimistic, pro-love clients. She couldn't risk going off the deep end and spewing anti-love slurs, offending clients. She continued jotting down her lunch order, adding mango margaritas. A few moments later, a rap sounded at her door.

She was so gonna fire Jordan. Or at least continue not to pay her.

The door opened and Jordan walked in carrying a crystal vase filled with what had to be two dozen roses. She closed her eyes. "I see a tall, dark, way sexy guy buying these flowers."

Omigod. Monica's heart raced. Her hands trembled slightly with apprehension as she opened a small red envelope and slid out a card bordered with hearts.

Je t'aime.

Her mouth dropped and she blinked several times, certain she was hallucinating.

Je t'aime.

That was all it said. And that said it all.

But did it? Did that suddenly make all their problems go away, or merely make them worse? The fact that they loved each other yet couldn't be together, at least not forever?

She separated the petals on a rose to find a small note written in red. *Je t'aime.*

Jordan peaked inside the rose. "What does that mean?"

Monica swallowed hard. "I love you."

"Ohhh," Jordan moaned. "I'm so gonna cry."

Monica and Jordan checked every rose, finding a note in each one. "What am I supposed to do?" she muttered, brushing a gentle finger over a soft rose petal.

"Oh gee, I don't know, how about telling him I love you, too? Kind of a no-brainer. And don't even try to tell me you don't." She gestured out the door toward the front window and Monica spied Reed's Mercedes parked at the curb. "So go tell him."

Monica's heart beat so hard against her chest she feared she was going to pop a button on her shirt.

Jordan handed her a rose then gave her a nudge. "Now go."

Monica twisted her mouth around in contemplation. "Suppose I should at least say thank you."

Jordan rolled her eyes. "A gorgeous guy says he loves you and you say thank you?"

"For the flowers, not for saying he loves me."

Reed *loved* her.

"I swear to God if you just tell him thank you—"

"We can't be together. It's never gonna work."

"*I'm* not gonna work if you don't at least go talk to him. I can't function in a place reeking of negativity. It'll suck the psychic juices right out of me. I'll—"

"Fine. I'm going."

Jordan gave her an encouraging go-get-'em nod.

Monica walked outside, a bundle of nerves, afraid she might vomit in the empty lilac pot. She noticed the Mercedes' license plate was missing and came to an abrupt halt. Wasn't it Reed's car? She slid a curious glance in the direction of his office. A new sign hanging over the door read *Reed Walker: Attorney at Law.* It no longer read *Family Law.*

What the . . . a hopeful smile slowly spread across her face.

Reed opened the door to his office and stepped out, wearing a lavender oxford and the same lavender tie he'd worn the night at the Casbah. He eyed the rose in her hand and a smile curled the corners of his mouth.

He gestured toward the empty lilac pot. "Does that mean the spell's been removed?" Stepping toward her, he held her gaze.

She stared into the blue depths of his eyes, trying to appear calm and collective when all she wanted to do was jump him right there on the sidewalk.

Did a changed *sign* necessarily mean a changed *man*?

She shrugged casually. "I was thinking *maybe* I want you to stick around. Really isn't fair to make you move before your lease is up."

He quirked a brow. "Maybe?"

"Uh huh," she muttered, sounding far from convincing.

He took another step toward her.

She glanced nervously down at the rose in her hand. "Thanks for the flowers."

"Thanks for making me a better man than my father."

Whoa. She hadn't seen that one coming.

"I swear I don't want to be like him, and I don't want to be a divorce lawyer. I'm thinking I need a more optimistic outlook on life." He eyed the empty pot. "I especially don't want to go away. I'd prefer to be closer." He took another step toward her, stopping mere inches in front of her, wrapping her in the scent of jasmine. "Much closer."

She nibbled at her lower lip. "You can get closer."

He slipped his arms around her waist, drawing her snuggly against him and she swept her hands up over his chest. He lowered his head and brushed a gentle kiss across her lips.

"You can get even closer than that," she said against his lips.

"I hope so because *je t'aime*," he uttered softly, lips brushing hers. "I love you." The warm words floated between her lips and into her mouth. She pressed her lips together, capturing the words, swallowing hard, wanting to keep them inside her. Her chest fluttered and her insides warmed as she imagined the words filtering throughout her body and becoming part of her, body and soul, forever.

Their mouths still touching, she parted her lips just enough to utter, "*Je t'aime*. I love you, too." She captured his mouth with hers, sharing the words, feeling their meaning.

He drew back slightly, gazing deep into her eyes, tracing a gentle finger down over her cheek. A contented moan drifted up her throat.

"You cast a spell on me I don't want you to ever remove," he said.

She smiled. "That's good, since no banishing spell could ever make us fall out of love. Nothing could."

Abracadabra. All it took was one Reed Walker sprinkled with jasmine cologne, wrapped in the color lavender, and blended with equal parts unselfish devotion and love to fully restore Monica's faith in love and happily ever after.

About the Author

When Eliza Daly isn't traveling for her job as an event planner, or tracing her ancestry roots through Ireland, she is at home in Milwaukee working on her next novel, bouncing ideas off her husband Mark, and her cats Quigley and Frankie. Learn more about her at *www.elizadaly.com*, *www.facebook.com/ElizaDalyAuthor*, or *www.twitter.com/ElizaDalyAuthor*.

CPSIA information can be obtained at www.ICGtesting.com
Printed in the USA
LVOW071908240213

321475LV00023B/1522/P

9 781440 557330